THE NEW WESTERN DOCTOR

THE NEW WESTERN DOCTOR

Book 1 A Western Medical
Fiction circa 1900-1930
Romance and Entrepreneur

Richard M Beloin MD

Rev. date: 08/14/2024

To order additional copies of this book, contact:
Xlibris
844-714-8691
www.Xlibris.com
Orders@Xlibris.com
861890

CONTENTS

AUTHOR'S DISCLAIMER

A Disclaimer

This is a work of fiction. Names, characters, business events, and products are all the result of the writer's imagination. Any resemblance to actual events, people, and locations are purely coincidental.

Some of my stories occur during well documented historical events such as the 1918 Influenza, WW1, the Roaring 20's, and so on. It is again coincidental that this story occurs during these times, but the story itself does not alter the historical facts.

DEDICATION

This story is dedicated to the doctors who interrupted their medical practice to join the military during wartime conflicts.

CHAPTER 1

Saving Addie

Brad was riding along the local river. He had a lot on his mind and it was time to make a decision. He was busy woolgathering when he heard a roaring sound that snapped him into reality. As his eyes gazed on the river he saw a woman frantically trying to stay afloat in a midst of muddy water with a wall of mud on her heels. Instinctively he pushed his horse into a full gallop down the river's edge as he came to a sudden stop, tied his rope to the saddle horn, slipped his gun rig and boots off and dove into the river with the rope in his hand.

Brad swam out into the river till he got to the end of the rope. He then turned around and saw a woman heading for his rope next to him. The woman crashed in the rope and fought to stay above water as Brad pulled himself to her and wrapped his right arm around her waist. Brad then yelled, "hold on to me and I'll pull us to shore!" The current helped as Brad swam with as much force as he could muster. When he reached shore, the woman collapsed out of exhaustion.

Brad picked her up and took her to a dry spot next to his horse. Holding her on his shoulder, she kept sliding off so he slipped his left arm between her legs, as immodest as it was, and used his right hand to pull out a blanket and towel out of the saddlebags. He then laid her on the blanket. Not sure if she was breathing, he placed his mouth on hers and blew three long breaths into her lungs. That stimulated her reflexes as she coughed and expectorated large amounts of muddy water. He then started to wipe her off with the towel and even had to clean her private areas caked in with thick mud. With the job done, he wrapped her in the blanket and started a fire next to her to finish drying her off and warm her up.

Brad then went to get his spare set of clothes, he stripped and instead of putting on the dry shirt and pants, he only put on his dry underpants and hung the wet clothes on nearby branches—while saving his spare dry pants and shirt for the nude lady. It took two hours before the lady was responsive. Slowly she opened her eyes, and asked, "what happened?" "I don't know, so you tell me."

"I was bathing in the river when the current took me away and a wall of mud was trying to roll over me. I swam away till I could only work on staying afloat, then suddenly I saw a light flash, and drove right into a rope and you appeared next to me. That is all I remember."

"Well that is certainly the sum of it, except I didn't think you were breathing once I got you on dry land; so I breathed in your mouth to add air to your lungs till you coughed up some muddy water and came back to life. After drying you up and cleaning the mud out of unmentionable areas, you finally warmed up and it looks like you slept the last two hours. Now that you are awake, what is your name and where do you live?"

"My name is Adelle MacFarland and I live on my ranch two miles out of Amarillo—everyone calls me Addie! And you are?" "My name is Bradley Kelly, I am from Dallas—everyone calls me Brad, and would you like a fresh cup of coffee?" "Yes I would and I need to get up!" Swinging the blanket off she said, "whoa, I am nude!" "Why yes, if you were bathing when the beaver dam let go, I can understand why you are still nude." "Well in that case, a wraparound blanket will have to do."

Addie got up, provided a naked frontal view and as she wrapped the blanket said, "so you caught a nude gal in the river, saved her from drowning, resuscitated her with mouth to mouth, wiped her body dry, dug out her private crack and flower, and all you have to offer me is a cup of coffee, why I am surprised you did not have your way with me?" "That is ridiculous, I would never do that without your conjugal consent; for proof if you check your flower/tulip you will find that you are still very intact." There was a pause as both started laughing.

After a welcomed coffee, Brad got up from his stump and went to get something out of his saddlebags. "Here you are Addie, my new replacement shirt, trousers, and socks with this old pair of boots That will do for now." Addie smiled, stood up, let the blanket fall to the ground, produced another naked frontal view and put the shirt on. To put the trousers, she sat on her stump, spread her legs, and slipped the pant legs on then jumped up to finish dressing. After adding the socks and boots, she walked up to Brand and gently slapped his cheek." "What was that for?" "For gawking at my privates!" She then kissed him on his lips. After lingering a bit, she said, "and that is for saving and taking care of me!"

Serving her a second cup of coffee, he asked, "you know that I am not a local, so tell me about you, your ranch, and this town." "Well I was born and raised on the ranch. My mom died of pneumonia when I was one-year-old. My high school years were a great time. I loved to work the cattle on weekends and I loved to learn. My dad saw in me, as far back as a child, the caring person I was. So he suggested that I apply to nursing school after graduation. With a law in Texas that stated, "any high school valedictorian was guaranteed admission and paid tuition in any state institution of higher learning. Well, as valedictorian of my class, I had chosen nursing school at Dallas General. That summer, my dad died of a heart attack while working the range. So, that turned my world upside down. I took over the ranch and had to decline admission to nursing school. And here we are, having coffee at your campsite, heh? So tell me about your past and what brought you here if you're from Dalas"

"Not much to it. My parents were both surgical doctors and spent their life teaching surgery at Dallas General. While in high school, my dad got me a part-time job as an orderly in the hospital. I enjoyed that and continued it after graduation while I took college courses. My parents passed away two years after my high school years. A couple months ago when the college courses finished, I had to decide what to do for the rest of my life. So I left Dallas on horseback and roamed all over north Texas trying to find myself. I was again wool gathering when I saw you struggling to stay afloat with a wall of mud trying to roll over you. And we have covered the rest of the story to now, heh?"

After a pause, Brad added, "with dusk soon to be on us, I think we need to get some supper ready."

"Yes, I'm hungry, what do you have for supplies?"

"Well you are in luck, I just restocked when I was in Amarillo. Not being the best of cooks, I stocked with easy to cook items. For tonight I have T-bone steaks, canned potato chunks to fry, bakery biscuits and butter, and canned peaches for dessert with all the coffee you want."

While Brad was frying the potatoes and heating the biscuits, he noticed that Addie was massaging her arm muscles and moving her shoulders and neck muscles. Brand said, "you may not realize it but by morning you will hurt in places you did not know existed. I bet you will have to lay low tomorrow to let your sore muscles quiet down, but we'll see by morning, heh?"

After a filling meal highlighted with two rare steaks, the Duo continued talking next to the campfire and under a moonlit sky. When it came to setting the sleeping accommodations, Brad said, "all I have is this bedroll and the blanket. Not to be out of respect, but I think we should lay the bedroll on the ground and then cover ourselves with the blanket—as we platonically end up sleeping together." "Sure sounds like a plan except for the fact that it is still 90 degrees and will be like that all night." "We can sleep in our underwear as I was when you woke up and I was waiting for my clothes to dry."

"Yeah, I remember that, and I also remember that you had a potato in your underwear's crotch." "Uh, that was no potato that was all me!" "Well then you must be hung like a horse!" "Yes, that has always been an issue to consider." As they dressed down, Addie totally stripped as she again exposed herself. Without a word from Brad. she said, "I don't have a choice, I don't have underwear, besides I always sleep in the nude—and that is not negotiable." Brad turned in while keeping his underpants.

As expected nothing happened during the night except when the sun came up. Brad was the first up and headed to the bushes. As he was emptying his bladder he saw Addie standing next to him. "That Mister Kelly is a manhood to behold and the difference between it and a potato, heh?" "As I said, and I shall never lie to you."

The Duo then dressed and started breakfast. Brad was cooking the bacon while Addie was frying the potatoes and both enjoying their first cup of coffee. While eating breakfast, Addie admitted she was somewhat sore from struggling with the water current. Brad offered her two aspirins and suggested that they take it easy today. Riding double would not be conducive to comfort while riding to her ranch. Addie agreed and asked, "what shall we do all day?" "There is a nice steam nearby and I expect we can find a nice fishing hole." "Great, fresh fish for lunch sounds wonderful."

The Duo went on a short walk with Brad's horse that held the two extra-large saddlebags. Finding the stream, they quickly came upon a large pool. Brad brought out some line and hooks as he cut down an 8-foot-long oak sapling. While setting up, Addie was turning over rocks and collected a half dozen worms. With a baited hook and a cork bobber at two feet, Addie walked to the stream and swung the bait into the water.

Within a short time the bobber disappeared as Addie started screaming; "I've got a bite." "Well set the hook and lift it up." Out of the water came a jerking 10-inch brook trout. Brad did the exchange and reset the hook. "Need three more for our lunch." Addie was having the time of her life as she pulled out another three. Realizing they had their limit, Addie was a bit embarrassed when she realized that Brad had not been given the chance to catch one. "Sorry, I didn't give you a chance to get one. I guess I've been the only child all my life and never had to make allowances for a sibling. Guess that cannot be the way with couples, heh?"

Brad was pensive as he added, "well that has also been my upbringing as the only child. I will admit that I had more pleasure watching you than I would have had doing the actual fishing. You have a mesmerizing and captivating deep laugh that vibrates my insides. Anyways, I'll clean the fish and keep them on a line in the water till we are ready to eat. Have a seat on that downed log and we'll dig a pit for the fire and make some coffee." "I'll dig the pit and start a fire."

Waiting for the water to boil, Brad asked, "yesterday you mentioned that, when in high school, that you had a dream of becoming a nurse. I know, out of necessity, you have become a successful rancher and businesswoman, but if the opportunity arose would you be interested in entering nursing school again?" "Hypothetically, if the opportunity ever came to pass, I would sell the ranch in a heartbeat. My neighbor Winston Holmes has already made two offers that were above the current market value. I would give my two ranch hands, Pedro and Berto Sanchez, a sizeable retirement fund, close the horse rescue when the horses were all farmed out, and walk away."

Brad paused and decided to push the issue. "That seems like a drastic change in your journey." "No it isn't, my destiny was planned a long time ago.

Taking the ranch over was a necessary deviation. Now after two years, I know that I am not meant to be a rancher." "But how can you be certain that a nursing profession is your destiny" "Because I have a lot of love to give, have a giving heart, and can encourage the sick and dying. Bottom line, I am a normal 20-year-old woman who wants a man, a family, and a caring profession!"

With the coffee ready, the Duo enjoyed the brew. To continue the conversation, Brad asked, "you are no booglin, you are a rather gorgeous gal, you appear alert, astute, and friendly; so you must have a man in your life?" "Well first of all, what is a booglin?" "Short fat and ugly!" "Oh well there must be hope for me, but no, there is no one in my life." "How come?"

"There are two reasons, the first is conjugal supremacy. There are very few men that will accept being 'secondo' to the ranch boss—it is easily perceived as a castrating position. Secondly, stepping out with single men is a humiliating and de-womanizing situation. For men today only want to fornicate or have their tanks drained—without any commitments. Those are activities that are reserved for couples in love and have commitments towards each other." "I see, well you'll get no arguments from me. Let's go for a walk?" "Sure."

Grabbing his double barrel coach shotgun loaded with OO buckshot, the two started walking along the stream. Addie was still thinking about their recent talk when she tripped in a gopher hole. Brad could not catch her in time. Helping her up, he then took her hand and said, "I am sure that your muscles have not yet recovered so hold on to my hand."

At the touch, something happened. There was a secure feeling that neither would ever be able to explain. Walking along, suddenly, a coyote was hot on the trail of a jackrabbit. Addie froze and said, "oh no, that rabbit has no defense—quick shoot the coyote." Brad pushed the safety off and fired. The coyote was dropped in its tracks as the rabbit made a turn to walk closer to its savior. To Brad's surprise, it came to a halt at Addie's feet as she bent down to pat its head. "You never cease to amaze me, wild animals never stop for a pat on the head. I can imagine what you could do dealing with sick people!"

Walking back to their fishing hole and Brad's horse, Addie kept looking at the pool. "I still need to bathe and wash my hair, do you have soap and shampoo?" "Yes, the soap is based on lanolin instead of lye and the shampoo smells like a chicken coop." "That's because it has egg white to make it suds up. Do you mind if I clean up?" "No go ahead." Addie never hesitated, before Brad could object, she stripped down and jumped in the water.

After soaking her hair, she said, "would you throw me the soap first?" "This soap does not float, and if you don't catch it, well better come and get it, heh?" Addie did not hesitate as she walked right out and gave Brad an uninterrupted full-frontal view. Grabbing the soap, she said, "you could have thrown it; you just wanted to get another look-see, heh?" "I'll never admit to it."

After scrubbing the dirt off, she asked for the shampoo. Brad, who had been watching all along, extended the bottle of shampoo. Addie automatically walked toward Brad, but this time did not exchange the soap for the shampoo. Instead she said, "Why don't you come in, you also have some of that mud still on you?" Brad did not speak, but dropped his shirt, trousers, boots, and socks. Walking in Addie added, off with the underpants, your member needs cleaning also, heh?" Brad hesitated since he knew he had a full salute on. Addie saw his hesitation and said, "we are both adults in control, and I have already seen your member in full salute since when you snore, your member responds with full turgor!" "Great, there is no secrecy even in deep sleep. Ok, but don't touch, heh?"

While Brad scrubbed the dirt away, Addie shampooed her hair. When it came to rinsing, she asked Brad to splash some water till the shampoo was gone. Laying back she immersed her hair as she again exposed her frontal view. Standing up, is when it happened. Brad put his hand on Addie's back, pulled her in, and kissed her in a long passionate encounter. Separating, Addie looked at Brad in a surprising amazement. "That Mister Kelly was not a peck, it was a statement." "Yes, I am developing feelings for you!" Addie's facial appearance changed to a satisfying smile, as she jumped in his arms and returned the passionate kiss. "Is there any doubt how I feel about you?" "No, you are very clear."

Walking on dry land, the Duo dressed, and sat on the log, but this time held hands. They talked about little things till the fire was ready and the Duo enjoyed their fresh fish lunch. The entire afternoon was spent talking and baking biscuits for supper. Several times Addie tried to find out what courses he had taken in college, but each time, Brad managed to skirt the subject.

There was one time that he almost spilled the beans when Addie asked how he had ended up in Amarillo. Brad was a master of switching subjects when he asked, "you've lived in Amarillo all your life so tell me about this town." "Well, have I got a story for you. Amarillo has a population of 1,500 residents. We have a great Main Street which houses all the merchants you need to make a living in town. We have a hardware store, a feed store, a butcher, several mercantiles, a gunshop, a blacksmith harness maker, an apothecary, three doctors of which two are in their 80's, a theatre, and town hall with regular dances, a courthouse, plenty of attorneys, a good sheriff, electricity, town water and sewage, carpenters, a town clerk, a garment store, and a dress maker. We even have a daily newspaper for a nickel, two hotels, and of course three saloons and three liveries. The bottom line, it is a great place to live and raise a family." "What is the major source of income?" "70% ranching, 10% services in town, and 20% railroad business. The town is becoming a major center for selling and shipping cattle to the major meat packers."

"Sounds like you are well supplied with services except for the medical care." "Yes, we have two docs that are mostly retired and one doc who works 80 hours a week, is near 50-years-old, delivers babies, does mostly general medicine, will treat gunshot wounds, and does one surgical procedure—an appendectomy under chloroform." "So you need more medical doctors and surgeons?" "Yes, especially since our population is expected to double in two years and be as high as 9,000 by 1910 as the rail shipping continues to grow." "Why is the rail cattle shipping expected to grow?" "Because we are 1,000 miles to the Chicago meat packers compared to the 1,350 miles from Dallas-Fort Worth to Chicago. With iced railcars, that 350 miles makes a big difference, heh?"

Brad paused and decided to push the medical topic. "What do you think is needed in a growing town as modern medicine is at our heels?" "As a woman, I cannot accept the high birthing mortality. We need an injectable medication or surgeons who can stop a hemorrhaging woman after delivery. Death in childbirth has to be controlled. I also cannot think of having a child that was delivered permanently damaged because we don't have a surgeon who can do an emergency Caesarian Section."

"What about other medical needs?" "To no disrespect to our Doc Morse, we need less elective surgery sent to Dallas to cover the 9-hour trip. Too much trauma does not survive because we don't have aggressive surgeons to intervene. And we need the new available medicines that no one seems to know exist. And last of all, it is time to bring childbirth into the hospital where surgeons are available for emergencies and for the new forceps deliveries."

Brad had heard enough as he added, "so you need a hospital instead of just doctor offices?" "Absolutely, but the problem is that we do not have the money in the general fund to build one—that would require an increase in the property taxes which would be a political suicide."

"Well, it has been an interesting afternoon, but with dusk upon us, I think we should prepare our supper." After searching the saddle bags, he said, "we have canned beef stew, coffee, and biscuits for supper. That leaves for breakfast—bacon, beans, and oatmeal with coffee." Addie looked at Brad and said, "that means we either resupply in town or we go to my ranch from then on, heh?" "Your ranch is my choice since a final separation can still be delayed or avoided!" "I like that."

*

After supper, the Duo prepared for bed. As usual, the bedroll was on the ground and the blanket was for cover. Brad stripped down to his underpants as Addie again went commando. This time, Addie turned to face Brad as the two held each other while they kissed passionately. After separating Brad said, "I am not sure what will happen when we get to your ranch, but one thing is certain, I am not riding out of your life!" The couple was beginning their roaming hands when Brad turned Addie around and went into a spooning position as he said, "goodnight." Addie was surprised as she expected more, so instead took his right hand and brought it to her breasts as both fell asleep.

Morning came early as Brad was busy preparing the bacon, beans, and oatmeal. It was a quiet time as he started thinking. *"If I am not riding out of her life, then it is time to 'fish or cut bait.' This is the woman who can be my friend, partner, mental match, lover, soulmate, and spouse. The question is whether I spread the news over months or hit the mule on the head and sink or swim."*

Addie finally stirred and after her morning ablutions she showed up next to the fire. Brad handed her a mug of coffee as she started to think. *"It has been two wonderful days. I am so comfortable with this man and cannot let him get away. I guess I am desperate and willing to make adjustments just to be with him. I finally realize that it can be painful joy to be in love."*

The meal was a quiet time. Afterwards, Brad said, "I guess it is time, lets pick up camp and I'll bring you home!" "Sure." After loading everything in the saddle bags and reburying the cat holes, the Duo stepped to Brad's horse. Seeing something wrong with the stirrup, Addie bent over to fix it. That is when Brad looked at her bum and could not resist as he placed both hands on her bum. Addie was surprised, straightened up and said, "whoa, what goes on here? Did I miss a message during the past two days?" "No you did not, but I finally realize that I can no longer resist you." As Brad moved his hands to her breasts and nibbled her ears.

After a passionate pause Addie said, "oh Brad, for two days I have been throwing myself at you, exposing myself, and considered seducing you. In those two days, I have developed such strong feelings for you that you could have had your way with me last night, but NADA—just passionate kissing and spooning. Why then and why now?"

Then they kissed as Brad said, "come and sit with me on the log. I have not been forthcoming with you and I need to clear the air. After pulling out a leather folder and straddling the log face to face, Brad pulled out a piece of paper. "At least three times in the past two days, you asked me what degree I had earned while in college. I avoided the answer till now, please read this carefully."

Addie read and turned as white as bed sheets. Out loud she said, "Bradley E Kelly has been awarded the degree of Doctor of Internal Medicine." After a pause she added, "oh my God, I have fallen in love with a DOCTOR!" Addie was shaking as Brad said, "there is more. Read this one." Addie silently read as she lifted her head and said, "you have been admitted to the two-year surgical program at the same school, the Dallas General. Oh my God, I am not inept but how can we plan to make a life together. This is an existential crossroad!"

To her wonderment, Brad handed her the third piece of paper. She read, "Admission document to the Dallas General Nursing program for physicians' wives." After another pause she said, "oh my goodness, you knew two days ago when you asked me the question about joining such a program!" Without a warning she said, "is this a proposal or what?"

Brad realized that Addie was about to decompensate as he dropped to one knee and said, "my darling lady. For two days I have been struggling with the idea of 'love at first sight.' Yes, it happened to me, after I gave you mouth to mouth breaths and you took a breath. At that instant I fell in love. After two days I now know that love is indelible and permanent. The threat of bringing you home and riding away brought me to my senses."

"Addie, I love you dearly. Marry me, become my wife, partner, my lover, and

we will work and live together. We will
spend two years in training together and
will go into practice together. All you
have to do is say yes and our destinies
will be secured."

"Oh my darling. In my entire life I have never
done anything without careful thought and planning.
Some couples take months of courtship to find love.
You took two days as I took one minute. The moment
I opened my eyes, saw you standing there in your
underpants with a potato in your crotch, I knew my
lifelong search for a man had come to an end. YES I
am in love with you, YES I want to be your wife, YES
I want to be a nurse, YES I want to be in training
with you, YES I want to spend our lives together.
YES, YES, YES, I will marry you!"

After passionate kissing and sharing tears of joy,
Brad dared say, "there is one more paper you need to
read. But let's get you to your ranch where we can sit
down and discuss this one in detail, heh?"

CHAPTER 2

Getting Things in Order

The ride to Addie's ranch took one hour. For the entire ride she held onto Brad, rubbed his chest, and often nibbled at his ears. When they arrived they went straight to the barn. There to their surprise, a golden Palomino stood at the barn door. Out came two elderly Mexicans. Addie stepped down and introduced Brad to them as her fiancé. Then she asked when 'Lady' showed up. "She got here five minutes ago, which was the first sign we had that you were in trouble." "Well Lady, you've been playing possum long enough, you need some 'stall' time, heh?"

As the Duo was picking off the saddlebags, Addie asked the men to go ask Winston and Ona Holmes to come over this afternoon. "Tell them to bring their bank book because I am selling the ranch! I will then settle with you two after the Holmes leave."

Walking in the house, Addie was quick to set some water to boil for coffee. In no time, the Duo was sitting together on the parlor's sofa. Addie looked at Brad and said, "you have my complete attention and I'm almost afraid to look at the last paper." "No this one is all good news; but before I show it to you, why are you selling the ranch?" "Don't you remember what I said about entering a nursing program." "Yes. but maybe you could hire a manager and keep it." "No, I want to concentrate on my studies and not have to wonder what is happening on the ranch. A complete severance is best, besides if we are both going to be in training, it takes money to pay for the training, room and board, as well as other living expenses." "Let's hold that thought about money, here is the last piece a paper that is a map and not a document. Take a good look and tell me what this looks like?"

Addie started scanning but quickly went to staring at different sections. "Brad this is a hospital?" "Yes, you are very astute, now look at the four different branches that spoke out from the center—the medical ward, the surgical ward, the maternity/nursery ward, and the doctor's offices, with smaller rooms for a casting room, a dental room, a laboratory, and an emergency ward off the center of the square with a reception counter at the square's entrance. The hospital is on 8 acres, plus those three side buildings is the beginning of 'Doctor's Row,' or housing for doctors on the adjacent 10 acres."

"But dear, that will cost a fortune, and who is going to work in there?" "Why we are dear, after our training, we are coming back to Amarillo to practice medicine, nursing, and surgery, heh?" "You promise me that after two years, we will return to Amarillo to make it our home?" "Yes, is that Ok?" "Oh yes, this is a perfect place to call home. Now are you sure this is the last piece of paper in that folder and there are no more surprises." "Yes, that is it, now let's talk about money." At that instant there was a loud knock at the front door.

In entered Winston and Ona, lifelong neighbors. Addie introduced Doctor Kelly as her fiancé, as Brad said they were getting married tomorrow at 1PM. Congratulations were extended as Addie added, "we will plan on leaving soon and I want to sell my ranch." Winston was first to speak, "boy, this is sudden, but I know that love works in many strange ways. Anyways, you know I need your 3,000 + acres and its good water. So I will make you a cash offer of $20,000 like I did a month ago." "No Winston that will not do. Your offer is too high. I have broken down the acreage, 200 head of cattle, house, and barn, and I come to $18,300. That is under one condition, that the rescue pasture for recovering horses is left in place till the last horse is picked up by the rescue association. Until then Pedro and Beto will stay here to take care of those horses. After the horses leave, which should be in two months, the guys will move to town for their retirement. Then you can tear down the fence or do what you want with that separate pasture."

"Deal, let's make a bill of sale, sign a release for the new deed, and I will give you your bank draft." "Great, then let's do it." Afterwards, as the Holmes were leaving, Ona asked "where is the marriage tomorrow?" "At the courthouse with Judge Gagnon or one of the 'justices of the peace.'"

With the Holmes gone, Pedro and Beto showed up as requested. Addie, after getting some cash out of her safe, went thru her directions regarding the horse care. Then she told them of their departure. "Move into town, take your hidden gold in the hayloft, and add it to this bank draft of $1,500 each. Handing them each $1500 she added, "this extra $300 in cash will cover your expenses till you find a home in town. Now tomorrow, go to town in the morning, open up bank accounts, take a bath, get a haircut, buy some nice duds, and be at the courthouse at 1PM sharp for our wedding."

*

Finally alone, Brad asked, "now can we talk about money?" "Sure, shoot." "I am a wealthy man. My parents were both doctors and taught surgery at the Dallas General Hospital for over 40 years. Other than buying a huge mansion they never spent a dollar. When they passed of an infectious fever, while

I was in medical school, they left their entire assets to me! So I sold the mansion, sold all their stock market investments, and with the bank accounts, I have over $100,000."

Addie was again flabbergasted when she said, "Brad Kelly, you are wealthy, why are we putting ourselves thru all these hoops to set up a hospital, go thru training, and go thru the woes of establishing a clinical practice. Why we could move to warm country, put our feet up, and drink tequila." "Would that make you happy?" "Heck no, we are both doomed to take the other road aren't we?" "Yes my love."

"So how do we divide the moneys, shall we keep your $100,000 to build the hospital and my $15,000 to live on while in training and starting a practice, or do we put everything in one account?" "We will be married tomorrow, so what is mine is yours and what is yours is mine. I just cannot believe that married couples should have separate accounts. That is not a way to share our lives and goals." "Ok, so I will put my $15,000 in your account?" "Yes, and your name will be added to my account and we will rename the account as 'Doctor and Missus Kelly, heh?'"

Sitting in the parlor the Duo did some planning.

1. This afternoon, load up the buckboard and bring Addie's personal items and clothing, in an old wooden crate, to the railroad storage.

2. Before returning to the ranch, stop at the garment store, buy a dress and a man's suit for the wedding; include one casual attire for the honeymoon.

3. Stop at the jeweler for Addie's engagement ring and the wedding bands.

4. Make a reservation at the local hotel for three days in the bridal suite and leave the new wedding and casual garments in their room— for the wedding and for changing the next day.

5. Return to the ranch for the night.

6. In the AM, make breakfast, close the house, head to town, and leave two trailed riding horses and a harnessed buggy at Joey's livery.

7. 8—11AM meet with Mike Walters—the carpenter.

8. 11AM make bank deposit and change names on the account.
9. 11:30 AM lunch at Waldo's Diner.
10. 12:30 PM change into wedding attire in the bridal suite.
11. 1PM arrive at courthouse for the marriage ceremony.

After a long afternoon in town, the Duo returned to the ranch. Addie was enthralled with her diamond engagement ring. Working together, they made a quick supper. Afterwards, sitting in the parlor, Brad asked if they were moving along too fast. Addie responded, "we did move fast to become engaged after two days, but it felt right and I have no regrets." "We'll have a busy day tomorrow, but then we'll have +- three days on our honeymoon." "So when do we head to Dallas?" "We have a week after the honeymoon to get registered and settle in our housing quarters. We can arrive anytime in those seven days."

As the time passed, the couple was beginning to get bothered, as Brad stood up and dragged his fiancé to the bedroom. Laying nude in each other's arms, both reached an orgasm without copulating. It was tender touching as they again reached their peaks together. After being spent, the Duo finally got a good night's sleep. They awakened early to draw their mutual baths and be up preparing their breakfast by sunup.

Arriving in town, the Duo brought their three horses and buggy to Joey's and made long-term arrangements for their storage and care. Next was the Walters office. Mike greeted them and said, "congratulations Addie, I hear you caught this man and getting married this afternoon." "Who told you that?" "Why Ona Holmes spread the word to a few ladies and the rest was history." "Oh well, no harm done, it is what it is, heh?"

Brad took over, "so where are we up to with the original design?" "Been working on it, and here is the master floor plan. Let's start with the Central Square, the four walls have an attached wing. At 9 o'clock is the Medical Wing, at 12 o'clock is the Surgical Wing, at 3 o'clock is the Maternity Wing with the nursery, and at 6 o'clock is the Doctor's

Wing of private offices. Each wing is 30 feet wide and 200 feet long. The additional sections along the Central Square, include the dental room. the casting room, the wound dressing room, the X-Ray room, the blood drawing/laboratory/transfusion room, the storage room. and the Emergency Ward (EW). The only wing and side room that has an outside entrance is the Emergency Ward."

Mike continued and described the Medical and Surgical wings. "Each wing has double rooms, one nurses station, and one pharmacy. The Medical Wing also has a 5-bed open ward. The Maternity Wing has two labor rooms, a delivery room, one operating room for emergency C-Sections, six post-birth rooms and an eight-bed nursery. The Doctor's Wing has eight private doctor offices and each with a treatment room."

The Duo was scrutinizing the layout as Addie asked, "where is the operating room?" "Right as you enter the Surgical Wing; it includes two operating rooms, a doctor's lounge, a nurse's room, an instrument sterilizing room, and a recovery room." Addie smiled and said, "nicely planned!" Mike added, "not my doings, this is all Doc Kelly's ideas."

Brad took over and said, "how do you propose to bring water, electricity, and oxygen lines to every corner of the building?" "Overhead drop ceiling with opening panels for repairs." Addie asked, "how do you insulate the walls if this is a brick building?" "Inside framing to hold wool drop insulation with paneled walls." "What is the heat source?" "Central kerosene furnaces with overhead air ducts next to the piping and wires."

There was a pause as Addie asked, "when a patient arrives, how is he or she directed to the hospital wings or doctor's offices?" Everyone who enters Central Square is met by the receptionist at the entrance counter. Those to see the doctors will wait in the waiting room till they are called, whereas visitors are shown where to go. Those to the Emergency Ward can enter without interference, and lastly, those who arrive for outpatient surgery will be gathered by the surgical prep nurse."

The Duo was tentatively satisfied with the early plans as Brad asked what the projected costs would be. "We can still erect the building with a finished rubber tile over concrete floor, brick building, insulation, and a steel roof for a $1.00 per square foot. So far we have approximately 30,000 square feet for $30,000. Inside partitions adds another $5,000, plumbing, electricity, and oxygen lines come to another $3,000, and toilets/ wash sinks another $2,000. Plus, $5,000 for beds and other accessories. So far, $45,000 is a likely fair estimate of the costs to build your furnished hospital, +- $5,000 for overruns, of course."

The cost did not seem to faze Brad as he added, "how much to build five private two story homes with an unfinished second floor along Doctor's Row?" "That will add close to $15,000." "Ok, so what deposit do you want to start the hospital project?" "$15,000 will do!" "Very good, when can you start?" "Tomorrow morning." "Well, here is a bank draft for $15,000 and we'll be here for 3 or more days to see you get started."

Addie added, "how long will it take you to have the hospital ready for occupancy as well as including the five doctor's residences?" "Finish work in the hospital will be very slow to be correct. This is an 18-month project to include private residences +- 2 months for delayed deliveries."

As the Duo left, Brad left an address at the Dallas General Medical Center for resident physician housing. "You can reach us at the center's telegraph office and we'll answer you the same day. Plus we will periodically spend a weekend day and come and see how things are coming along."

Their next stop was the bank. President Rankin was surprised to see that Addie had sold her ranch. Amidst the surprise the bank president almost let the cat out of the bag but recovered in time. Brad saw the slip up but let it pass as 'brain freeze.' "So how may I help you?" Addie said, "add this $15,000 to my account and transfer the balance to my future husband's account." Brad finished as he asked that Addie be added to his account and to change the name of the account to both Doctor Bradley Kelly and Adelle Kelly.

Being done with the two important errands, the Duo went to Waldo's Diner for lunch. Waiting for their hot chicken sandwich, Addie asked, "I was amazed at the hospital layout, you seem to be adding new things to medicine." "Well, it is time to add certain things if we are going to move medicine and surgery into the 20th century. In actuality it is time to add doctors' offices in the hospital along with a diagnostic laboratory, an Xray department, blood typing and transfusions, an insulated dental extraction room, a casting room, an Emergency Ward, an anesthetic nurse, an obstetrician, an official nursery, a multi suite operating room, instrument sterilization, surgical gloves, surgical garments, a modern medicine pharmacy, intravenous solutions for fluids and electrolytes, and start a bank of blood typed donors for transfusions. As you can see, there is so much that is needed to get medicine out of the post-civil war era."

"Yes, I can see what we will be faced with. In the same line, do you have any idea which surgical procedures you are planning to do in this hospital?" "Yes, based on the surgical curriculum, these are the operations that are currently performed at the Dallas Medical Center and the ones I would be expected to perform before leaving the institution. They are: mastectomy, appendectomy, cholecystectomy, bleeding stomach ulcers, vagotomy, colon resection, colostomy, pneumothorax thoracostomy, hysterectomy, hemorrhoidectomy, nephrectomy, hernia repairs, circumcisions, C-Sections, ectopic pregnancies, open fractures, and generalized trauma including gunshots—to name the basics."

"Oh my, that seems so much to learn, doesn't it?" "Well I am told that repetition is king as you will eventually live by the saying, 'see one, do one, and teach one.'" "Well let's hope so." With their food arriving, they ate in silence.

After lunch, the duo went to their hotel room to change into their wedding outfits. Delaying things with some gentle touching, they eventually were ready. Brad looked at Addie in her white dress and all he could say was, "my God Addie, you look like a goddess, how did I ever get so lucky?" "You set up a barrier with a rope tied to you and your horse; why I never had a chance to resist, heh?" "Yep, there you were in the flesh, and I mean flesh—one tall curvy and lanky beauty."

After a short walk, hand in hand, the Duo arrived at the courthouse. The clerk seemed a bit nervous to arrange for a wedding till he said, "the judge has decided to perform the ceremony. So step into his chambers to do the preliminary paperwork to fill out duplicate marriage licenses."

Opening the door to the judge's chambers, Judge Gagnon stood and came to greet the Duo. "Welcome Addie, and we finally meet Doctor Kelly. For your info, Mike Walters is my son-in-law and he told me about your plan to build a hospital in our community. That is very noble of you and I thank you. But now we have a marriage to perform." After signing the necessary papers, the Judge said, "follow me to the courtroom where the witness is located."

Walking in the courtroom the judge hesitated as he raised his voice and said, "welcome folks to the marriage of Adelle 'Addie' MacFarland to Bradley E Kelly MD. Walking in, the Duo nearly collapsed, as they saw a courtroom full of clapping smiling friends, merchants, cattlemen association members, cattlemen, and the proud organizers--Winston and Ona Holmes.

Once the guests sat down, Judge Gagnon started the proceedings. "Friends we are gathered here …" "Do you Adelle, promise to … and do you Bradley promise to … and with the power invested in me by the State of Texas, I now pronounce you man and wife. You may kiss your bride."

*

Once the congratulatory applause started, Winston was quick to announce, "you are all invited to Waldo's Diner for a wedding reception in the special party room. It includes liquid refreshments and a special hot roast beef meal off one of my beefers. See you all for the festivities starting with the reception line to hug and kiss Addie, and meet the Doctor."

It was a short walk for all to reach Waldo's party room. The reception line started and Addie was busy introducing Brad to the many locals. "Brad, this Frank Tisdale from the hardware store, this is Merton and Delia Merchason from our grocery, this is our mayor, Ulysses Monroe, and this is our sheriff, Sheriff Sam Butler. Of course you know Joey, Judge Gagnon, President Rankin, and this is our doctor, Ephrain E Morse MD." "Yes, I know the doctor." "These are my high school classmates with some husbands—too many to name; and of course all the other merchants plus the many cattlemen that I have done business with. The last was the Holmes. Brad addressed an issue, "please tell me the costs of putting on this meal so I can pay for the expense?" "No way, we have known Addie since she was a baby, and when it came to the ultimate change in her life, she called on us to buy her out. That Doctor is worth all the money this meal can cost. Consider it, your wedding gift, heh?"

Beer and wine flowed freely as Winston called for the newlyweds to the head table along with Winston, Ona, Judge Gagnon and Sheriff Butler. After the usual clinging of spoons against water glasses, Winston called for 'grace' as Waldo appeared with the beef hind-quarter and started slicing either rare from the center or medium from the edge. When all were served, the meal proceeded with baked potatoes, carrots, beef gravy, buttered rolls, and plenty of tea or coffee. After the wedding cake was served, Winston stood and asked for a speech from the newlyweds.

The newlyweds stood and Addie started, "for the past week I have had many surprises thanks to my loving husband. This surprise also tops them. I shall never forget your consideration. Now it is time for you to learn who Doctor Bradley Kelly really is. " Bradly got up and said, "I have a message in two parts: a story and current plans."

The Civil War had just ended and two high school sweethearts were graduating in your high school; that was the valedictorian, Zebulah Kelly, and the salutatorian, Amanda Fuller. The couple went on to medical school at the Dallas Medical Center. After getting their MD, they stayed on as surgical instructors for the next 35 years. Unfortunately, they passed a year ago from an infectious fever as I was in my second year of medical school. I graduated the third year as 'Doctor of Internal Medicine.' That summer I came to visit the small town where this all started, Amarillo."

"That brings us to now. I spent two weeks in town and spent many hours with Doc Morse, Mike Walters, Mayor Monroe, and President Rankin. Being my parents' only heir, I inherited their sizeable assets. To get to the chase, I have purchased a +- 15-acre plot of land on the edge of town and I have negotiated a construction price with Mike. Starting tomorrow he will start the construction of your first hospital—The Kelly Memorial Hospital in honor of my parents, Zebulah and Amanda Kelly." The party room erupted with unbelievable commotion.

When the guests settled down, Brad said, "there is more! Addie and I will be leaving soon because in one week, we will be beginning a two- year-training at the Dallas Medical Center. Addie will become a general nurse with specialty certification as a surgical technician and surgeon's assistant; as I will be getting certified as a general surgeon." There was more applause. "But there is more, after our training we are planning to return to Amarillo and start a surgical practice in the Kelly Memorial Hospital." More eruptions and applause. Brad then finished by adding, "if things go well in Dallas, being a training hospital, we hope to bring with us more doctors that could be useful in this community, which is expected to double in size within our two years in training."

A question-and-answer session automatically started. "How long will it take to build?" "18 months." "Who will occupy it till you arrive?" Doc Morse got up and said, "I will!" "Is this going to be a one room hospital or will it be divided into different section?" "It will be divided into four major wings: Medical, Surgical, Maternity/Nursery, and Doctor's Offices. Plus it will have several small treatment rooms and the first official Emergency Ward. May I add, there will be many innovative ideas and it will bring modern medicine, as we know it today, to your community. We will keep you all posted as the construction proceeds thru your local newspaper. So look for the serially informative articles, heh?"

Winston then got up and said, "that is it for today, it is time for the newlyweds to leave for their private honeymoon. Thank you for coming."

The newlyweds walked to their hotel. Arriving in their suite, Brad was all over Addie. Suddenly he said, "There is no doubt that we will consummate our love and marriage several times but you must not get pregnant. We both have two crucial years that will affect the rest of our lives. As much as I want a family, I do not wish to see you with child during the next two years. I know you are a bright person and capable of anything, but carrying a child is not reasonably in the cards for now." "But I want to consummate our love, so what are we to do. Are we to service our needs as we did last night as we celebrated our engagement?"

Brad said no. "We need to practice safe sex except two days before and after your monthly cycle." Brad then went thru the explanation how to practice safe sex. At the end, Addie said, "but if you withdraw after I reach my peak, before spilling your seed, where does that leave you?" "That is my sacrifice and my choice. But like last night it leaves me in your hands, heh?"

With Brad's determined control, Addie had a quick orgasm after their copulation and Brad was able to withdraw in time. Addie was pleased to have reached her first orgasm and made sure that her husband was well taken care of. The night was long as the newlyweds made use of every possible moments. By morning, the newlyweds who had not eaten since the wedding, were ravenous. After a mutual bath to wash off the sexual sweat, the Duo went downstairs for their first rejuvenating breakfast.

The honeymoon lasted two more days and nights. For two days, the couple only left their room for meals in the hotel's restaurant. Years later they realized that those two days in solitude had solidified their inseparable relationship. It was Addie, who the third morning, said, "we are now truly husband and wife and it is time for us to meet the monster face to face. We need to get to Dallas, and settle in before our training starts. If we are lucky, we can purchase some required textbooks and get acquainted with them, the school, and our neighbors, heh?" "For sure, you are right. Let's purchase some new traveling clothes, some training attire, and get to the railroad for our trip to Dallas."

CHAPTER 3

Training Starts

After doing their shopping for garments, they sent a telegram to the Dallas Medical Center training office informing them of their arrival tomorrow to register in the physician surgical and nursing program for physician wives. Loading their railroad crates, the Duo took a two-meal program for their expected 8-hour ride to Dallas. Having left at 6AM, the Duo was expected to arrive by 2PM—plenty of time to register in the training center's admissions office.

The trip was upbeat as several businessmen were from Amarillo and knew of the future local hospital. The time flew by between breakfast and a late lunch. By the time lunch was done, the conductor announced, "arrival at the Dallas terminal in 10 minutes."

Taking a terminal taxi to haul their luggage and railroad crate, the Duo was quickly dropped at the appropriate admissions' office. The taxi driver came in with the Duo and once the secretary told the driver, Unit #11, he said that their luggage and crate would be left at their Unit #11 doorsteps.

"Good morning Ma'am. We are Doctor and Missus Kelly, here for official registration in the surgical and nursing program for physicians' wives." "Yes we have been expecting you. Have a seat and I will check to see if the department heads are ready to see you."

Walking in the inner sanctum, the Duo was introduced to Doctor Karl Huxley and Master Nurse Kravitz. Doc Huxley started, "well Doctor Kelly, you had the summer off and you come back with a wife, heh?" "Yes, and a wonderful and intelligent lady to be my office nurse and surgical assistant." Nurse Kravitz adds, "our records indicate that you were valedictorian of your high school class but that you declined admission to take over the family ranch. So what is different now?" "I have sold the ranch and my dream never died to become a nurse. Then meeting my husband, well things were quickly solidified. Here is my information sheet and our marriage license signed by the local district judge."

Doc Huxley enjoyed the banter between two powerful women, but had an official registration to perform. "Very good, shall we proceed. The fee for two training programs is $4,000 plus books. It includes:

1. Housing for married couples—two room apartment with full water closet.
2. Three meals a day including weekends.
3. Four uniforms per person. The ladies have dresses, head caps, and hair cover for the operating room. The surgeons have surgical scrubs with head gear. This includes a laundry service at the uniform office.
4. Barber and hairdresser service. Nurse Kravitz adds, "we recommend that the ladies have a short hairdo because of the intense program and frequent long hair management—but not required. However, long hair will need to be rolled up and retained in place."

5. Medical care and maternity benefits.

6. Books depend on the electives and are extra expenses. So Missus Kelly what is your plan?" "I will do the 4-phase program. That is six months each in General Nursing, Office Nursing, Operating room technician, and surgeon's assistant—and in that order." "And Doctor, what is your plan?" "18 months in general surgery and six months in trauma." 'That will be spread as 12 months of general surgery, six months in trauma, and the last six months as senior resident that will allow you to do your own operations and have your wife start learning how to be your surgical assistant." "Yes Doctor, that is greatly appreciated." "So Missus you get four textbooks, one for each section of your choosing. Doctor you get four as well—general surgery, anatomy atlas, gun-shot wounds, and a large text on the '15-operation technique' on these specific procedures we expect you to learn. These eight texts will add $40 to your final bill. Get these books in the bookstore."

"That about does it except wear your clip-on ID. You have four days to walk about and get accustomed to the place. Check out our store for several items you might use on campus—at your expense of course. Since these training programs are so intense, we offer two things for relaxation. We have an inside heated pool at your disposal, and the Saturday night supper can be eaten in the dance hall where a dance follows after the meal. Generally, unless you are assigned to the emergency room, Sunday is your day off, and we do have a nondenominational church service at 11AM. Last of all, surgical residents have 24-hour access to the anatomy lab of bodies donated to our training program, and that includes nights and Sundays." On leaving, Addie handed Doc Huxley a bank draft for $4,000.

*

The Duo walked to their apartment while holding hands and porting a satisfying smile. After entering, they quickly checked the place out. The kitchen included a dining table and the remainder of the room was a parlor with two comfortable chairs, a sofa, and a double ended desk for studying. The only other room was the bedroom with a double bed, two dressers, two night-tables, and a walk-in closet. The other two side rooms were a utility room and a water closet with a shower and a two-person tub. Other amenities included electric lights, two gas heating stoves, and a small triple propane burner in the kitchen. After the tour, Brad grabbed Addie and was all over her. "My dear husband, we have other things to do before supper. Let's hold our hormones and let's unpack."

The new garments went right in the closet. Addie who had brought her entire life's belongings did some selective unpacking. Most clothing items made for ranching went into the dumpster as did all her high school clothes and books. By the time they finished, only items useful in the next two years were stored in their apartment. It being 5PM, the Duo headed to the hospital's cafeteria. Showing their clip-on ID, the Duo went thru the line. Addie selected a meatloaf dinner as Brad took the rare roast beef dinner. Sitting down a couple came over and said, "we are your neighbors at #10, may we sit here?" "Why of course!" On the other side was a gal who said, we are your other neighbors at #12." "Well have a seat!" To their surprise another couple arrived and said, "we're #9 as there is no #13, heh!" After the Duo introduced themselves and mentioned their chosen training curriculum, the others followed suit.

#12 Tom and Sally Greene; Surgeon—office, OR tech, and assistant.

#10 Daniel and Ingrid Hall; Pathology/laboratory—nurse anesthetist.

#9 Stanley and Cindy Norwood; Obstetrician—labor and delivery nurse.

So their meal started. The Duo was familiar with everyone's chosen field except for Daniel. When asked, he said, "pathology includes tissue histology, gross tissue identification, laboratory blood analyst, phlebotomy, blood group identification, IV infusions, blood transfusion,

X-Ray technology, and when necessary inhalation anesthesia. In other words it's an accessory discipline to make a hospital functional." After the meal was done, the Quad lingered. The four men were all MD in internal medicine and now specializing before going into practice. Closing the cafeteria, the Quad agreed to meet again late tomorrow afternoon at the indoor pool.

The evening was short as the Duo was early to bed. After their first union, Brad was wondering why Addie was so quick to peak and have her orgasm. "As you copulate with me, you overfill me because of your size. So I get distended and engorged. I then cannot resist an instant peaking and experience an amazing orgasm. So it is what it is, and I'm not complaining. Until we can copulate freely around my monthly, I am not expecting any changes." After repeated copulations, the result was the same and Brad added, "feel fortunate, for some women never experience orgasms." "Well I am convinced that your gigantism has a lot to do with it, heh?"

The next morning after a shower they went to the cafeteria for breakfast. During the meal, Addie said, "we need two things. We both need swimwear and I think we both need a haircut." "Are you saying you are cutting your long hair?" "It would go along with our new beginning but only if you approve. Brad paused and said, "to think of it, we'll be taking two showers a day, one in the morning to wash off the sex sweat and one when we get home to wash the smell of embalming fluid in the anatomy lab or the smell of human bodies in surgery. So let's start our day in the barbershop/hair-dresser shop and see what style they have to offer us."

Sitting in the waiting room Sally came out with a short haircut. Following her was Tom with a man's stylish short haircut. At the sound of "next" Addie said, we'll have one of each of those cuts. After a satisfying result, the Duo went to the hospital's store. Brad chose some boxer trunks since the 'speedo' type just exposed his excessive manhood. Addie was torn between a two-piece versus a one-piece. Brad liked both and said, "take one of each, you know how gals like to vary their attire."

Shopping around, it was clear that dancing couples tended to wear the newest style of outfits. So the Duo purchase three of each. Their last purchases were quick breakfast item of sliced bread for toast, jams, peanut butter, and instant oatmeal. For an afternoon snack they included soda crackers and cheese; for a bedtime snack they bought sugar cookies. The most important purchase was several pounds of Arbuckle's ground coffee ready for the percolator, and sweetened with honey or sugar. Picking up some note pads and writing materials, the Duo went back to drop their goods off in their apartment and then went for a late light lunch of a half egg salad sandwich and cup of potato soup.

Back home, Addie tried her swimsuits. Brad almost fell off his chair when Addie came out in her two piece. "Whoa, you do look like a goddess. You do realize the panty barely hides your crack and the top piece only covers half your breast and is on the edge of your nipple." "So this one is too revealing?" "Not for me or any men, and if you have it then flaunt it. All that matters is that I am the only one who ever sees what that two-piece covers. Till we see what the other ladies are wearing, maybe you should wear the one-piece unit."

Addie changed and Brad said, "better cup size and more breast is covered. But dear, the crotch shape of that suit shows too much of your hair. I need to give you a trimming shave." "Yeah, I figured you'd find a way to get your nose close to my love button. Just be careful with your blade, there are some precious pieces down there that make my motor run, heh?"

*

The afternoon was a revelation. The heated pool was in a glass building heated to 90 degrees year-round and the water temperature was kept at 88° F. The shallow end was 4-5 feet and the deep end at 8 feet. There was a diving board only 2 feet off the water. A refreshment/snack bar was open noon to 5PM. Swimming laps were allowed only on the lengthwise edges. It was a relaxing event with 'noodles' to keep people afloat while socializing. At one point, Brad mentioned to Tom, "I cannot believe how many beautiful women are in the medical profession." "Yeah, it's a good thing we are married to two beauties because I just don't think I could work the field anymore!" "Heck, with my wife, I have no such urges as well. But they are certainly scantily clad aren't they?"

As the afternoon passed, Addie asked, "so where are you all from and why come to Dallas Medical Center for specialty training?" Daniel said, "we are both from Austin originally but I did my medical training here. I met Ingrid as a nurse's aide in a nursing home. Now she wants to be a registered nurse and specialize as a nurse anesthetic. We left Austin because it was too hot and born Texans always get trained in Texas, heh?" Hearing that, Stanley said, "Cindy and I are both from McAllen Texas on the Mexican border and it really gets hot there. After three years in Medical School in Dallas, while Cindy worked as a waitress just to pay our way, now we are getting trained in the cooler Dallas area."

That is when Addie added, "well we are from Amarillo Texas where the weather temperature varies between 50 in the winter and 85 in the summer. Two years ago we had six inches of snow." Brad could not hold back as he said, "and that is an 8-hour ride by train to Dallas."

By 4PM the group agreed to get changed and meet at the dance hall at 5PM for supper and a dance. When asked what type of dancing, Addie said, "when in Texas, it's the Texas Waltz and Two-step, heh" Once in their apartment, the Duo rinsed off the chlorine, and got dressed in dancing clothes. Brad kept saying they had time for a quickie, but Addie knew better.

Arriving at the dance hall, the other three couples were already sitting at a table for eight. The Duo arrived as Sally said, "newlyweds always arrive last, heh?" Brad could not resist, "if that is true, then why don't it feel like I got away with something? "

After a chicken and dumpling supper, the band started. Realizing that both Brad and Addie had learned to dance, the Duo had never danced together. Getting on the floor, Brad got in the mood of a rhythmic two-step and Addie had no problem following his lead. After the dance Addie looked at him and said, "you never cease to amaze me as you are a great dancer." The evening went well, and the intermission was a great socializing time. By the last dance, Addie knew that Brad was getting in distress while dancing the last waltz of the night. When the band stopped, Brad whispered in Addie's ear, "wait till I get you home, heh?"

Arriving at their apartment, the Duo was undressed before they even got to their bedroom. Brad then said, "you tried to mount me during the last dance, well now there is no clothing barrier, so mount up and impale yourself. Addie never hesitated, she jumped in his arms, wrapped her legs around his hips and dropped herself on his full tumescence. As usual, she started peaking after full penetration. Except when she lost control, at the height of her orgasm, she nearly fell to the floor. That was the beginning of a fantastic night of true love and release.

The next morning, the Duo stayed in and had toast, oatmeal, and coffee for breakfast. Regaining their strength, they then took a walk to the bookstore to get their textbooks. They each found their four assigned texts as Brad saw other texts that might be useful when in practice but decided to wait till his training was in progress. After walking around, Brad made a bank draft for $40. On their way home, they stopped at the uniform office to get Addie's dresses, white coats, and scrubs for all.

At the counter was a typical Mister Gruff. Addie went first, "I will be in nursing and my specialty will be OR technician and surgical assistant." "Ok, give me your measurements." Bust size 34 DD, waist 26, hips 34 inches, inseam 32." "And shoulders end to end." "No idea." "Turn around" as the attendant drops a measuring tape from point to point and says, "20 inches." He then disappears and brings back armfuls. "Here you are Missus, 5 dresses, 5 nursing caps, 5 head gear, 5 surgical scrub tops, 5 scrub bottoms. Remember the rule, wear one, one in your locker, and three spares at home. Here is your women's locker number #29 with two keys. Lost keys are $1 apiece."

"Now what about you Doctor?" "Chest size 42, waist 34 inches, and inseam 32 inches." "That will be medium top and pants at 32 inseam." Returning from the storage area, he had 5 tops, 5 bottoms, 5 surgical caps, and two keys for men's locker #44. "Same rule, wear one, one in locker, and three at home. All your dresses and scrubs are coded to your name. Laundry is picked up daily and clean ones placed in your mailbox within 48 hours Monday to Saturday." "But you don't know our names?" "Doctor, I have been here 45 years, and I know a Kelly when I see one—and welcome back Doctor, with a beautiful wife no less, heh?"

That afternoon, the Duo spent time going over their texts. After a general perusal even Brad had to admit, "it's going to be a lot of work to learn all this. Addie agreed but shocked Brad when she said, "It appears that general nursing and office nursing has a lot of common sense. I am planning to cover that in six months, and the next six months will be to learn to be an OR technician with the many surgical tools I will need to learn. That will prepare and free me up for our second year when you will be in trauma as well as a senior resident, and I can be your assistant in the anatomy lab and in the operating room." "Yes, I agree that accelerating your program will better match with my surgical training."

The next morning the Duo went to church services at 11AM. Afterwards, the Quad went to lunch in the cafeteria. Sitting there, everyone was a bit anxious and somewhat hesitant to eat or even speak. It was a serious matter to enter into such a rigorous educational program made worse by arrogant surgeons or strict nursing instructors who knew better than anyone else. Brad summarized it by saying, "It is only a bunch of hoops, we'll all get thru them, and will be properly trained to take care of people's lives—to alleviate pain and maintain a quality of life. Actually we were lucky to be chosen, so hold up your heads and accept the responsibility, heh?" Tom yells out, "here—here!"

*

After a memorable night between happy lovers, the Duo dressed in medical garb. Addie looked like a queen in her well-fitted dress as Brad looked like a well-seasoned surgeon. Although they had planned to meet for lunch, things got hectic and never made contact till they got home. After closing their apartment door, they greeted each other like the lovers they had become. After some serious pandering, the Duo sat on the couch and Addie started describing how her day went.

"DRESSINGS, DRESSINGS, AND MORE DRESSINGS. I never would have thought that Nurse Kravits could talk for 8 hours and never repeated herself. Dry dressings, wet dressings, purulent dressings, infected sutures, draining wounds with drainage tubes, detritus appearing at a lesion, bandages sticking to incision or sutures, wounds opening with stuck gauzes, hydrogen peroxide to the rescue for caked in gauzes, mangled dressings, contaminated incisions, and on and on." While filling the percolator, she continued her rant. "I know everything about dressings, when to call in the doctor for problems, suspected infected wounds or surgical incisions, and always schedule dressing changes when the doctor is doing office hours and is available between patients. Tonight I have to remember exactly what is in a dressing tray and then review how to do a sponge bath on bedridden patients." Brad wondered how she would describe washing a man's member and sac. Instead she appeared with a soapy bucket and started washing a resentful husband—"ARE YOU LISTENING AND WHAT IN BLAZES ARE YOU DOING?"

"You are a madwoman. Intense all the time, heh? Well I am unbuttoning this dress from neck to floor. Then I am going to take you while you are standing— you need to relax and so I am going to give you a deep protein injection." "So if I come home ranting and raving, you are going to sedate me, heh?" "Yes Ma'am, a service of mercy." "Then proceed!"

Later while enjoying a fresh cup of coffee, Brad went over his day. "KNOTS, KNOTS, AND MORE KNOTS. All day I tied knots: square knots, surgical knots, double hand, single hand, at skin level, medium wound depth, deep wound depth, instrument ties with needle holders or Kelly forceps. Heck, I will still be tying knots in my sleep."

There was a long pause as Addie asked, "is there anything wrong with you teaching me how to make knots, seeing that I will eventually be your surgical assistant?" Brad also paused when he pulled out a roll of 1-O silk and said, "I was just waiting for you to ask. How about if we start with the basic two-hand square knot. We'll anchor it on your nipple, heh?" "If we do that, the second knot will be on your member's tip, and tight enough to turn it blue, heh?" "Oh boy, it is going to be a challenging two years."

That night, sitting at their desk, Addie memorized the dressing tray, not to forget the safety pin, and practiced the two-hand square knot. Brad was studying the list of surgical tools and said that their second day would be learning the name of each tool and what it was used for. Addie realized that tomorrow night would be another busy night. By bedtime Brad said, "do you realize how much we learned in our first day, can you imagine how much we will learn in two years?" "Yes, a bit frightening, heh?"

The next night, after an overwhelming greeting, the Duo started working on the surgical tools. Brad had brought home a sample of each tool and the variation in sizes for each. "This is a Kelly forceps or clamp and it comes as curved or straight in three lengths, and with or without striations—and used for ... ! The second one is a hemostat in one size and is used for clamping on a bleeder till a suture is tied on the bleeder. Addie handled both and then said, "ok, what's the rest called and what they are used for?" "Well we have:

- Tissue clamp
- Surgical probes
- Handheld and self-retracting retractors
- Surgical scissors, curved, angled, and straight for cutting sutures
- Scalpels—four designs
- Needle holders—regular or long
- Surgical needles, straight, curved with or without cutting edge
- Skin suturing hooks
- Curettes

"And of course there are sutures but that is for tomorrow night. Now let's review their names and we'll discuss their uses another night after I have had the proper instructions. Before I forget, this is a standard surgical pack that is opened for each operation. Now for specific operations, a specific pack is opened. As examples, there are specific kits to include: chest, abdomen, and pelvic kits. To be even more specific a cholecystectomy procedure would have three opened kits—standard, abdominal, and gall bladder kit. More on these later."

There was a long pause as Addie committed each name to memory.

Afterwards Brad asked how Nurse Kravitz handled washing a man's member. "She just said, 'either you wash your privates or I will do it for you.'" "Yep that will usually work. But if it is not possible, how would you do it?" "As Nurse Kravitz said to use our judgement. So I would muckle on, lift it up and wash it just like it was a dirty sink with a faucet and drain hole, heh?"

The next night, Addie had learned how to take vital signs. Finding a pulse was a challenge but that blood pressure machine was interesting. So Addie came home with an oral thermometer and a BP cuff. After taking his oral temperature she tried to entice him in using a rectal thermometer but Brad declined. After taking Brad's blood pressure from both arms at least a dozen times, Brad said, "one more time and I am going to put that cuff around your neck and pump it up."

After supper in the cafeteria, the Duo went back to their apartment and Brad went over the sutures currently used. "We have absorbable and non-absorbable. The non-absorbable include cotton, silk, and stainless steel. The absorbable include catgut and chromic catgut." "Now I understand cotton, silk, and steel, but what is this catgut?"

"Catgut is made from sheep's intestines—that is the collagen on the outside wall. It takes about 7-10 days to lose their tensile strength and fall apart. By adding chromium to the catgut you make chromic catgut which will hold tensile strength for 10-14 days.

So it is important to know when you cannot use dissolvable sutures. Now the sizes of all sutures are as follows:"

NAME	SIZE IN MM
3	.6-.9
2	.5-.6
1	.4-.5
O (1-O)	.3-.4
OO (2-O)	.3-.35
OOO (3-O)	.2-.25
OOOO (4-O)	.15-.2

"I am sure you realize that it is up to the surgeon to request the proper type and size, so don't open any suture ahead of time. Now I will add the presentation of the four surgical blades that is used in our operating rooms. They are the #10,11,12, and 20. The number 10 is the long universal blade with a rounded belly. It is used from the skin to the organs till the procedure is done. #11 is straight and pointed and is useful when making specific short cuts. #12 are like #10 but curved and are used when cutting hard fascia and cartilage. #20 are longer and larger than a #10 blade and is used in slicing tissue specimens for pathological study by the surgeon or pathologist."

The next day was hypodermic injection day for Addie. "We were told that only doctors gave injections. So Nurse Kravitz discussed preparing an injection and how to fill a syringe with extra air in the medicine bottle. She also explained that most needle used was the 1 ½ inch 22-gauge needle for intramuscular injections. Then she shocked us all when she segregated the nurses who would be office nurses and told us we needed to know how to do intramuscular injections. So loaded with an empty syringe, we shot up apples for hours. Then to shocked everyone as she had me, Addie Kelly, inject her with ½ ml of saline. Well let me tell you mister, I shoved that needle almost to the hub and took the mandatory 5 seconds to inject the ½ ml of saline. Then she shocked me again when she said to Sally and Ingrid to inject my right and left deltoid. It was a real memorable day I assure you." Brad was almost on the floor listening to her ranting and raving.

At the end, Brad did note that needles ran between 16 gauge for IV cannulation, to 25-gauge 5/8 inch long for children and subcutaneous use in adults.

It was Saturday when the surgical instructors reviewed their week's work and took questions from the new residents. The same was done by Nurse Kravitz. By 3PM, the Duo was home early, sipping on coffee in their parlor, and totally amazed at what they had learned the first week.

Brad was especially proud of Addie who had learned both systems. It was agreed that this knowledge, for political reasons, would not be shared with anyone else at this time. By 5PM the Duo was sitting with friends and waiting for their meatloaf meal before the dancing started.

*

Sunday became the mandatory rest day. The Duo got up late, had breakfast at home, went to church services, had lunch at the cafeteria with their friends, and spent the afternoon reading ahead either in their parlor or at the pool.

Over the next weeks the Duo was exposed to daily new subjects as some were more memorable than others. CPR was high on the list as Addie had no idea that such a technique could save lives. Brad had learned it in Medical School but the technique already had been revised several times. It was now two breaths followed by 15 compressions that depressed the chest wall 1.5-2 inches—hopefully generating a pulse.

Another subject that was popular was how the operating room people sterilized instruments and surgical garb. The instruments were exposed to boiling water for 30 minutes or steam for 15 minutes. Dry heat was another method which included 320° F for 2 hours or 375° F for 6-12 minutes. The old method of soaking the instruments in carbolic acid was often used as it was also customary to soak surgical towels and gauze sponges in the same phenol solution. Under current research was a quicker sterilization of instruments and surgical cloth by using steam under pressure as the temperature of steam would increase from 212° F to 350° F (soon to be called an autoclave).

Week after week, the Duo was exposed to daily new subjects. It was now the end of the first month and the Duo had been exposed to daily new subjects for a total of 26 days plus off on Sundays. To their surprise, Brad was now graduated from the operating room balcony observation tower and was finally in the operating room even if only the third assistant or the first surgical live observer as was known to all new residents.

Addie had whisked thru general nursing and the office nurse minimal requirements as the doctor's official helper. She was now entering the hospital setting as a med/surg nurse while working the hospital wards.

For the Duo, it was now 'make it or walk away' time!"

CHAPTER 4

Early Ward and OR Days

Addie and the dozen first year students were standing in the medical ward as Nurse Kravitz said, "there are more patients than nurses. The registered nurses have two or three patients and you will be assigned to one nurse. Your job is to help them do whatever they ask of you—no matter how disdainful some jobs can be. So in this ward we have three patients with pneumonia that not only need nursing but also chest therapy. We also have six stroke victims that need a lot of hygiene, ADL's (activities of daily living), and exercising the stroke extremities. There are six patients with CHF (congestive heart failure) that need many epinephrine and diuretic injections. There are two MI patients (myocardial infarction or heart attack) that are heavily sedated that need total care from hygiene to help feeding them. And the most demanding are the three liver failures in DT's (delirium tremens) from alcohol addiction." There was a pause as it was clear that each nursing student was deciding which patient they would volunteer to provide care. Nurse Kravitz put an end to this process when she said, "in a month's time you will end up caring for all these patients and the new ones that get admitted. So to avoid confusion I will assign each of you to one nurse/patient team that I will change every two or three days. Sally you have the heart attacks, Ingrid you have the congestive heart failure, Cindy you have the alcohol addicts that need a lot of that foul smelling paraldehyde medicine, Addie you have the pneumonias to do chest therapy and the rest of you have … for the next three days. That is it. Introduce yourselves to the nurses caring for those patients and we will have a Q & A at 3PM before you go home. I will be walking around all day and guide you if necessary."

Addie introduced herself to Myrtle, "hi, how can I help you?" "We need to do drainage and chest percussion on my three patients every hour. So I will start by showing you what to do. First cup your hands so. When you tap the chest there is a sound wave that penetrates the chest wall and ends up in the lungs. There it helps the lung secretions to loosen up and start flowing out. With the patient's head of bed being down, gravity helps the outward flow of the purulent secretions. Watch." The percussive tapping had a classic sound. As Myrtle was tapping away, the patient started coughing and the secretions started expectorating into the emesis basin (kidney dish). "There, now it is your turn. Remember, not a closed hand, use a cupped hand." Addie started and quickly got the hang as she heard the classic sound. The patient responded. After five minutes, the patient was turned on his right side, then the treatment repeated on the left side. The entire treatment took 15 minutes and they repeated the same on the second and third patient. That left 15 minutes for actual nursing care as the entire process started on the second hour.

The lunch break was an edifying event. Several nurses could not eat and several spent their time losing breakfast. Addie was glad to eat as her arms were sore from the physical treatments. That afternoon, one of Addie's patients was producing an excessive amount of secretions. Myrtle told Addie to draw up 1 mg of epinephrine in a 5/8-inch 25-gauge needle, and give the patient a subcutaneous injection to cut down the secretions. Addie drew up the medicine, showed the syringe and bottle to Myrtle and went ahead with the injection without any hesitation.

The sickest of the three pneumonia patients had an accident and needed new sheets as well as get a sponge bath. Addie said, "go ahead and start the next chest therapy, I will take care of this, heh?" After the necessities were finished, Addie went to wash her hands and returned saying, "all is well, let me take over and take a break." It was that time when Nurse Kravitz was walking by and Myrtle gave her a 'thumbs up' as Addie was pounding away. Addie never saw Nurse Kravitz as she smiled and placed a checkmark on her clipboard.

3PM arrived as the Q & A started in the classroom. Several nurses had complaints about nursing duties not always being dignified for ladies. Nurse Kravitz had an answer ready, "one day you might be ill and some nurse will be there to wipe your mess. That is when you realize that there are angels after all. Yes, you are angels, so if the shoe fits, then wear it gracefully! If you don't agree, then make a change before you become bitter and end up treating the sick badly."

After more appropriate clinical questions, the meeting was about to close when Addie asked, "I was surprised when my nurse could not answer why the patient's doctor had ordered certain medicines or treatments. When I asked why she did not ask the patient's doctor why he had ordered such treatments, my nurse said," 'why it is not the custom for nurses to ask such things to doctors.' "Is that true?"

Nurse Kravitz paused and then said, "the times are slowly changing and when you will be dealing with surgical residents, you will get an answer as these modern doctors want the nurses to know what they are ordering on their patients. The problem is the old guard. Many of the attendings are of the old school and they have never explained things to the nurses. It's been like that for years and will only change during the next generation of doctors. You nurses need to use diplomacy and respect the old guard for their time in medicine is limited. The young doctors will notice your respectful behavior and that will reflect on the way they deal with you. Confronting old doctors will get you nowhere and as the saying goes, 'honey will attract more flies than vinegar, heh?'"

*

That evening, Addie went over her day treating pneumonia patients by doing chest drainage and percussive treatments. Addie added how her feelings for Nurse Kravitz were changing each day. "Not only does she know nursing technique, but she is actually a very caring person." When Brad's turn came up he said, "my day started seeing an Upper GI bleeder in the Emergency Ward. The patient was in shock and with the second- year resident, we started an IV, gave him a liter of saline, and gave him a transfusion by blood type specific blood. When the attending arrived, emergency surgery was ordered. That is when I learned what surgeons go thru to be ready to start an operation."

"First we washed our hands, scraped our under nails, lathered up with an iodine soap, and then took the brush and scrubbed our hands and forearms for 5+ minutes. Then rinsed up and held our arms up, backed into the OR door and stood there with hands at face level till a nurse in full garb handed us a sterile towel to dry our hands and forearms. Then the nurse draped each surgeon with a gown from front to back as the OR supervisor tied the cord in the back. Then the nurse opened our gloves so we could shove our hands in them. Then we all stood there with our hands on our lower chest till the attending surgeon snapped his gloves and the operation started."

"The carbolic acid-soaked towel was removed from the patient's abdomen and a surgical sheet with an open surgical window was draped over the patient. The attending surgeon was standing on the patient's right and the second-year resident was across the attending as I was next to the resident and the OR technician was next to the attending directly across from me. The attending asked for a #10 blade and made an eight-inch incision four inch above and below the navel—and the blood flowed PROFUSELY."

"The two surgeons were applying hemostats to clamp off the bleeders as the OR technician was handing them as fast as she could. Once hemostasis was achieved, one surgeon was holding the hemostats while the other was tying off the bleeders with 2-0 catgut. Afterwards, the 'attending' made several more cautious cuts and entered the peritoneal cavity. The resident then exposed the stomach as the 'attending' again made a swift cut in the stomach and exposed the cavity full of blood. The resident then inserted a suction tube and emptied the blood out. The exposure quickly revealed the ulcer with a central pumping vessel which the resident clamped off with a small, curved Kelly forceps. The 'attending' tied the artery with a 0-cotton double surgical knot. Then the team oversewed the ulcer with a purse string #1 cotton suture. The resident was then given the nod as he sutured the stomach closed with 2-0 cotton sutures. Before they closed the abdomen, the resident identified the vagus nerve and performed a vagotomy to decrease stomach acid production. Then the resident sutured the abdominal wall fascia and re-apposed the muscles and fascia with two #3 silk retention sutures. At the end I was handed a curved cutting needle with 2-0 silk and told to make stitches every ½ inch. I then applied a dressing secured in place with experimental surgical tape used in the Medical Center. At that instant I knew that soon I would be that second-year resident, and during my second year I would eventually become the attending surgeon before I left this institution. Brad then said, "Addie, I was hooked for life—a surgeon I would become or die trying for the drive in me is beyond an existential issue."

*

Addie was a curious soul who wanted to know what medicine could or could not do for any disease. So after treating pneumonia, she took Brad's old textbook on Internal Medicine. Reading became a disappointing exercise since there were no treatment with medicines that could kill the causing germs. There was only chest therapy, oxygen, intermittent epinephrine injections, and other supportive measures. So over the month spent on the medical ward, Addie read the internal medicine text on each condition that she encountered. After the month she amassed a disappointing list:

1. Heart attack (MI). Morphine for pain, nitro for chest pressure, oxygen in early phase, heavy sedation with barbiturates. It was an attitude of turning off the lights, closing the door, and hoping the patient was alive in the morning.
2. Congestive heart failure (CHF). Continuous oxygen, oral digitalis, intermittent muscular mercurial diuretic injections, salt restriction and maintaining a low body weight.

3. Stroke. In medicine it was considered an elderly patient's blessing. Many strokes were fatal but gave the family time to say goodbye. Those that lived needed major family support to deal with their disabilities. There was no medical treatment except support and the affected extremity exercises to prevent contractures.

4. Diabetes. Low carbohydrate diet, lose weight if overweight, stay active. Wait for insulin therapy which is years away.

5. Emphysema and asthma. Adrenergic bronchodilators, intermittent epinephrine injections.

6. Alcohol withdrawal. We can treat the DTs with paraldehyde but no treatment for liver damage or cirrhosis.

So Addie worked her entire month in the medical ward. She learned as much nursing techniques she could on the ward but twice as much at home reading the text on internal medicine. It was the last week on the medical ward when Addie was caring for an asthma patient when the patient went into an extremist state. Addie was sent to the pharmacy room to get some epinephrine. As Addie walked in, she found Nurse Kravitz being set by a doctor. Both were at their peak but Addie ignored them and grabbed the epinephrine as if nothing had happened.

It was days later when Nurse Kravitz addressed the issue, "well Addie, what are you to do about my indiscretion? An official complaint will lead to my dismissal." "There is no way that this institution is going to lose a great instructor and an ethical nurse—I saw nothing. Now on a personal level, I am not the one to judge people. I do recall that during my single days, that every day I had a painful yearning for a man. Now that I am married, I am as content any women can be. I will never deny any women the right to feel like I do—just choose a better location to satisfy your needs. With your master key, the locked custodial closet is a safer location, heh?"

The last days spent on the medical ward were spent discussing with Brad the lack of medicines for non-surgical diseases. Addie was saying, "the treatment of medical conditions is still in the post-civil war days. With all the new surgical procedures you have, why is medicine lagging?" Brad was serious when he said, "it seems that medical research comes from the far advanced hospitals in the eastern US. There is not enough money spent on research until the demand increases. We can only treat patients with the medicines we have. It behooves all doctors to stay current when new drugs come out, as they shall year to year."

*

Brad had been patient during his first month as the second assistant or first observer, or master retractor holder. The observation days had been fruitful. Brad had ordered a dozen anatomical pictorials on the most performed operations in the medical center as well as a half dozen pamphlets on gunshots. During operations it was customary for the first assistant 2nd year resident, or the attending to ask questions—as in a 'one upmanship' hierarchy. Brad had spent the evenings reviewing the operations and was usually able to answer their queries with factual responses.

It didn't take long for Brad to realize that the more he could answer their questions, the more he was allowed to do during the operation and the more the surgeons would discuss their technique.

By the end of his first month in the surgical ward, Brad was being scheduled as first assistant for minor procedures and getting to do a lot of knot tying and applying sutures. It was at that time when Brad was the second assistant on a cholecystectomy. The gall bladder full of stones had been removed and Doctor Davis was about to start the closing when Brad suggested that the common duct should be probed for leftover stones. Doctor Davis looked at the first assisting 2nd year resident and asked him what was going on. The resident was truthful when he said, "I was not given the time to review this patient's history and lab tests. But I can assure you that when our sound Doctor Kelly speaks, we all listen." The attending was an older surgeon who was not always aware of modern discoveries. Doc Davis said, "hu'um a Kelly, heh? That figures. Well step aside and let the great Doctor Kelly move forward. Here is a probe, now tell me if you are correct. Brad takes the instrument and carefully probes the proximal end of the common duct and found no obstruction. He then probes the distal end and finds a firm obstruction. "Yes, I believe there is a common duct stone obstructing the flow of bile."

Doc Davis did a double take, repeated the probing himself and confirmed the finding. The attending's words were clear, "well Doctor Kelly you are right, be proud that you saved that man's life. So would you do the honors and pull that stone out. Nurse, give Doctor Kelly a small-curved Kelly forceps." It was later that Doctor Davis asked Brad how he knew there was a residual stone in the common duct. Brad said, "the blood liver tests showed an elevated alkaline phosphatase and a high direct bilirubin—hallmarks for biliary obstruction." Doc Davis smiled and said, you saved me from embarrassment and my career, and that will never be forgotten. Plus I will start scrutinizing the patient's chart before surgery, heh?"

*

The second month of clinical ward duties found Addie in the surgical ward. The first day, she was impressed how illnesses were addressed with a definitive surgical procedure. The nurse's duty was to help the patient get thru post-operative care. That meant the care of tubes in the abdomen, urinary catheters, chest tubes to water bottles for air trapping, IV tubing, IV bottles, blood transfusions, and draining wound care.

Along with the mechanical contraptions, was pain management. Fortunately for Addie, she became very adept with the hypodermic needle since intramuscular morphine injections were the mainstay of pain control in the immediate post operative period. Later, aspirin, phenacetin, and acetanilid were the oral mainstay in pain control unless oral laudanum was needed.

Addie was first exposed to other post-op methods. Compression leg dressings for maintaining circulation, the control of edema, and postulated other necessities such as anti-embolism. Yet the most important experience was in learning the many complicated surgical dressings especially the ones with drainage tubes for expected infections with certain injuries. All in all, her time spent on post-op care was well spent.

Brad's second month in surgery was a quickly progressing one because of his encounter with Doctor Davis. The word was spreading around that Brad was a hard-working thorough doctor, had some natural surgical talents, and was a reliable physician to take on cases that uppity doctors would shun. Week by week, his skills were put to the test.

The month of November was busy and the Duo saw their first break at Thanksgiving. The nursing and surgical residents were off for four days. The Duo celebrated the holiday as the Quad had Thanksgiving dinner at the cafeteria with other nursing and surgical residents. After the holiday, the Duo sent a telegram to Mike informing him of their coming visit. The Duo was then on the first train to Amarillo to see how the hospital's construction was coming along.

*

Being pressed for time, the Duo took the overnight express and arrived by 9AM the second day of their vacation. Mike was waiting for them at the terminal as he drove them by buggy to the hospital. On arrival, the Duo was struck as if smacked on the head with a pole ax. There in front of their eyes was the brand-new brick building complete with a steel roof, windows, and doors in place.

As they stepped inside, Mike said, "winters are unpredictable, so we wanted to be enclosed by Thanksgiving. We are totally sealed up and have temporary coal heating stoves to handle the cold season. We have tons of work to do this winter so I decided to hire sub-contractors—to include professional services in plumbing, electricians, and heating ductwork. They will all be starting next week and my carpenters will start insulating the brick walls and adding the interior walls. I expect that we will be installing the pipes, wires, and ductwork till next spring and insulating interior walls may take as long."

The Duo then took a walk and were surprised to find five wings instead of the four that was originally planned. Brad said, "so what led to building a short fifth wing?" "You can thank our Doc Morse for that.

He's been checking our progress each week. He asked one day where the patients and the working staff would get their food. I said, "why in the kitchen and cafeteria, of course." Doc Morse added, "well then you had better find space for those rooms or add another wing." Three days later he showed up with another question." "Where will the patient and worker's laundry be located?" I answered, "why beyond the kitchen and cafeteria, of course. Doc Morse left with a smile on his face and the words off his tongue, "just keeping you on your toes." "Actually he has been a big help as he has sound practical judgement."

After more inspections and review of the blueprints, Mike added, "I hate to pull this on you, but several providers of medical equipment have been bugging me. Apparently medical equipment comes from unique state of the art manufacturing companies, and a six months to one year wait is not unusual. The salesmen for such equipment come from Austin and I have already arranged for them to be here tomorrow at 10AM in my office. If everything goes well we will order what is needed in the doctor's offices and treatment rooms, the fracture room, the operating rooms, the sterilizing room, the nursery, the delivery room, the kitchen, the emergency room, operating room surgical tools, the medical and surgical ward beds, and miscellaneous medical equipment." "Fine we'll be there at 10AM and bring our bank book, heh?"

It was a celebratory evening mixed with a fine supper in the hotel's restaurant, a nice mutual hot soak in the tub, and a night of sexual ecstasy. By morning the Duo elected to call for room service to deliver their full breakfast. By 10AM they arrived at Mike's office where the three salesmen were anxiously awaiting. The Duo caught the salesmen's first names, Walter, Roger, and Dexter—the 'er' Trio. Then came the specifics to match a 50-100-bed hospital with the necessary expenses:

1. Alloyed carbon steel kitchen. $500
2. Cafeteria tables and chairs for 50 staff $100
3. Private doctor offices X 6 $300
4. Private doctor treatment rooms X 6 $300
5. Fracture room, table, tools, plaster $200

6. Operating room tables—two $200
7. Sterilizing room—steam and dry heat $150
8. Nursery heating incubators—two $150
9. Delivery table—two $200
10. Labor beds—two $100
11. Post partum beds—8 $150
12. Medical ward beds—25 $500
13. Surgical ward beds—25 $500
14. Bed mobile side rails—50 $400
15. EW stretchers—six $150
16. Laboratory, chemistry analysis, blood typing, H &E staining kit, histology and dissecting microscope. $500
17. Surgical instruments
    Standard kits—4 $400
    Chest kits—2 $100
    Abdominal kits—4 $200
    Pelvic kits—2 $100

TOTAL $5,200

Brad looked at the bill and said, "Shall we say $9,000 since I know we will need much more as the building starts filling up. Why don't we authorize you gentlemen to add anything we will need to function in the doctor's offices and in the hospital." Addie already had the bank draft written out into three equal parts of $3,000 for each salesman.

Next, arrangements were made to store these orders in Mike's warehouse as they would likely arrive at different times. After another night of hotel luxuries, the Duo finished their vacation and took the next train back to Dallas. After arriving, the neighbors greeted them and wanted to hear the details of how the hospital was coming along. When all three couples were told that the building's basic brick framing was already enclosed, their facial appearances changed. The clincher was hearing that they had ordered all the basic necessities from hospital beds to surgical tools to the tune of +- $5,000 and left a deposit of another $4,000 for future necessities.

Returning to work till the Xmas holiday revealed two events that changed the lives of both Addie and

Brad. It all started with Addie when Nurse Kravitz was assigning patients. Addie was last when Nurse Kravitz said, "I have conferred with the surgical nurse supervisor, and we both believe that you are ready to be your own patient care nurse. So I am assigning you to Mister Starr who needs treatment for an infected wound and Mister McCutcheon who just had an emergency splenectomy. He has lost a lot of blood, has received two liters of saline during surgery and is now getting his first of two transfusions. He is in a lot of pain, has post-ether excitation, and needs a morphine injection."

Addie went to her task. After quickly assessing McCutcheon's vital signs she noted that his BP was borderline low, but his heart rate was too fast at 128 bpm. Figuring he needed the morphine, she started drawing it in the syringe when her patient started seizing—which Addie recognized as a cardiac seizure with impending death. Instantaneously she swung her right arm and slammed her closed fist onto the patient's sternum. The seizure stopped but without a pulse. Addie then jumped on the bed, straddled his right arm and started with chest compressions. After a dozen or so compression the patient opened his eyes and lifted both arms trying to stop Addie from pushing on his chest. Addie got caught with the patient's fist up her dress to her crotch. She yelped but managed to free herself.

McCutcheon's first words were, "what did you hit me with and why does my chest hurt so. As McCutcheon was looking at the floor, Addie asked, "what are you looking for?" "For that sledgehammer, heh?" "Sir let me explain. You just had a cardiac arrest and were dying. I hit you with my fist to perform a 'precordial thump' to stop your cardiac seizure and then I provided cardiac massage till your heart restarted. I did all that because NO ONE DIES WHILE UNDER MY CARE. It may be true that I may have broken a few ribs, but you can recover from that and besides the morphine I will give you for your painful incision will take care of your chest wall 'bobo' heh?"

McCucheon paused and finally said, "are you sure that I am safe here?" The nursing supervisor was standing by and said, "Sir you are safe in this hospital and you are obviously in good hands with nurse Kelly. Addie continued to care for her patients right up to five days before the Xmas vacation, while on her way home she stopped to pick up her mail. In the mail was a note from the Director of Surgery requesting her presence at the surgical council meeting at 3PM the next day.

*

It had been two weeks since Brad returned to work. He had recently had the opportunity to be first assistant surgeon and was feeling good about it. It was a busy day when Brad was assigned to the Emergency

Ward when a young sickly appearing man presented with abdominal pain. Brad obtained the medical history, performed an exam, did some basic labs, and called for an attending surgeon.

A well-known surgeon by the name of Doctor Davis appeared. "Well Doctor Kelly, we meet again. We have certainly had several encounters lately. So what do you have today?" Brad started presenting the case as Doc Davis was looking at the chart. "So what is your diagnosis?" "Acute appendicitis, and presumably before an abscess has had time to form or just starting."

Doc Davis added, "I see the blood count has high white cells with mostly neutrophils. You see, I have learned since the case with the bilirubin and the common duct stones, heh Anyways, I agree, let's call for an emergency appendectomy."

While scrubbing, Doc Davis asked, "so where does this McBurney's point come from? A pioneer surgeon in the late 1800's by the name of Charles McBurney pointed out the exact point on the abdomen which was over the appendix. Pain to palpation is characteristic of appendicitis and is the location to make the surgical incision." "Where did this surgeon practice?" "Roosevelt Hospital in New York City." "Well at least it wasn't in England!" "So is appendicitis deadly?" "Yes, until we have medicines to fight off infection it will remain with a very high mortality."

"So doctor, are you ready and have you reviewed the procedure for an appendectomy?" "Yes, I am very familiar and have assisted in several with other attendings." "Very good, shall we enter the OR?"

With both surgeons draped and gloved, Doctor Davis draped the patient, snapped his gloves, and asked for a #10 blade. Without hesitating, he handed the blade to Brad. "Doctor, this is your case and I believe you are ready to perform your first complete operation. I shall be here to assist you!"

Brad deftly made the incision at McBurney's point, clamped and tied off the bleeders, separated the muscles, and entered the parietal peritoneum. He quickly located the appendix with a tiny abscess beginning to form. He carefully placed a sponge under the appendix, then doubly clamped the stump with two small-curved Kelly forceps. Cutting between the two Kelly forceps he gingerly lifted the infected appendix to a kidney basin. Afterwards he applied the carbolic acid to sterilize the stump as he adeptly inverted the stump into the caecum (colon). The last step was to carefully apply a 2-0 cotton submucosal purse suture to close the entrance to the caecum (colon). After closing the peritoneum, muscles, fascia, and subcutaneous tissues, he applied a subcuticular running suture of chromic catgut to the skin, thereby avoiding sutures removal in the future.

At that point Doc Davis yelled out "Voila, that was a perfect operation and Doctor Kelly's first solo procedure." Doc Davis started the applause as the other surgical team members followed suit. High in the observation was a proud Addie with tears down to her chin. As the surgeons were heading to the Doctor's lounge, she stepped forward and kissed her husband and said, congratulations, I knew you could do it!" Once in the lounge, Doc Davis handed Brad a certificate of completion for an appendectomy with a 10/10 rating. "Well Doctor Kelly that is one down and eleven to go before you graduate as a practicing surgical attending. Keep up the good work and I know you will get there, heh?"

It was a week later when Brad got the same note from the surgical board asking for his presence at the council meeting. That evening Addie was a nervous wreck. "Why does the surgical board want to see us. We haven't done anything wrong so why summon us?" "Who knows and who cares, all I care about right now is making sure you reach your peak, now concentrate, heh? For I seem to be ahead of you which is not good."

When 3PM arrived, the Duo was in front of Doctor Huxley. "Well as you can see, I wear different caps. I am the admission officer as well as president of the surgical board. Now I was shocked that a first-year resident would get certified for an appendectomy after four months of training—and a 10/10 rating. To complicate this, I have just been handed a second certification for hemorrhoidectomy by Doctor Colon. It seems that you are not afraid of volunteering for the not so popular operations and you are exhibiting some talented natural surgical moves. So congratulations— that's two down and ten to go!"

"Now let's get back to why you were both summoned to this meeting. Missus Kelly your medical and surgical supervisors in cahoots with Nurse Kravits have requested that you be granted an exception and allowed to move ahead to the OR nurses level just about 8 months ahead of schedule. Are you ready and willing to accept this advancement?" "Yes Doctor, it has always been my goal to train to be an OR nurse to hand the surgeon's tools, as it will also bring me closer to learning how to become a surgical assistant." "Very good, then the council secretary will notify the OR supervisor that you will begin your advanced training on January 3, 1904.

"Now Doctor Kelly, I have in my hands four letters of recommendation requesting that you be prematurely advanced to 2nd year surgical resident only four months since your surgical training started. Do you believe you're ready for such a responsibility. The next step is becoming an attending and that is a life and death responsibility."

"Doctor Huxley, it would be easy for me to just say yes to your question but there is more. I feel comfortable in the operating theatre. It is part of me and I don't know why. All I know is that I am confident in my technical ability and I am certain that if there are any attending hesitations they will confront or correct me in time."

"Very well, since the board has unanimously voted in your favor, you will also start as a 2nd year resident as of January 3rd. The board is adjourned and congratulations to both of you. Here are your new name tags, 'Adelle Kelly OR Nurse' and 'Bradley Kelly MD Resident #2'. Wear them proudly because you have both earned them."

CHAPTER 5

Premature Commitment

That same evening, the Duo was having supper with the other three couples. Congratulations were abounding. The discussion turned to the Xmas day celebration. The three couples made it clear that they could stay on campus for the holiday or take a train trip to Amarillo to see how the Kelly Hospital was coming along. That was when Addie kicked Brad in the shin and although it took a while, he finally came around.

Brad finally said, "In the same line, Addie and I have been wondering if you might be so inclined. Since you are, this is what we are offering you as a holiday gift. The day before Xmas Eve, take the train with meal services to Amarillo. We will put you up in the 'Queen Amore Hotel' and include your meals in the hotel's restaurant. On Xmas Eve we will meet with our contractor and you'll get a tour and all your questions answered. Xmas day, we will have a private party in the hotel's small party rooms. Your total cost will be zero because we will pay for everything. This will be a business write-off, heh?" There was little discussion as all six friends were looking forward to the adventure out of Dallas for a change.

At midnight, the Duo took the 'overnight red eye' to Amarillo. They needed to get to the town's high school by 11AM to meet with the senior girls who would be graduating in May.

Addie started the meeting by saying, "Some 3+ years ago I graduated from this high school. After two years as a rancher, in another year, I will be a Registered Nurse, a certified OR Nurse/technician, and eventually a surgeon's assistant. It can be done and it is a permanent profession. Now let me present my husband Bradley Kelly MD."

"Ladies, if you marry, will you be able to supplement your family income?" Pause. "If you don't marry, will you be able to support yourselves?" Pause. "If you were unfortunate to become a widow, would you have a training to support yourself and your children?" A final pause. "That is why we asked for this meeting."

Addie added, "you all know we are building a hospital. That means we need ward nurses as well as specialized nurses. One year of training is what you need to become a Registered Nurse who can work in a physician's office or in one of three wards— medical, surgical, or post-delivery. Doctor Kelly will get down to specifics."

"The Dallas General has such a nursing school. It starts this September and runs till mid-August. The cost is $1,000 to include tuition, room and board (three meals a day), books, and uniforms. You could technically enter the school without a penny in your pocket and come out a year later as an RN— assuming your registration fee of $1,000 is paid."

After a pause Brad added, "we are offering you gals a special deal. If you apply within the next three months and are accepted, we will pay all your expenses." Applause. "In addition you will all receive $25 each month for personal items and for a few luxuries to include coffee and a snack of crackers, peanut butter, and jam while in your housing quarters. Yes, we will pay all your expenses under one condition. That you promise, without a written contract, to come back to Amarillo after your training and work in our hospital for two years—under current wages and not a payback for the $1,000 we advanced you—that was free money." More applause and many oohs and aahs.

"Some of you wonder why I said to act in the next three months. Well by April there is a 50/50 chance that the class might be full, and by your graduation, the class will be full and you would lose an entire year floundering in town."

Addie then added, "if you were to stay in training after your RN degree, to spend another 6 months and $500, you would become a specialized RN such as a labor and delivery nurse, an OR nurse, or a nurse anesthetist. Plus if you add another six months and another $500 to an OR nurse, you can become a surgeon's assistant." More applause and cheers.

Brad took over. "Now let's talk about wages. Considering that the minimum wage for factory workers in Texas is $500 a year, or a biweekly(BW) wage of $19.23; let's talk about your wages. An RN working the wards will get $1,250 a year (BW $48.08). A specialized RN will get $1,750 a year (BW $67.31). A RN surgeon's assistant will get $2,250 a year (BW $86.54). Plus everyone gets medical insurance and a one weeks' paid vacation or 7 single days off with pay." More applause and loud cheers.

After a long pause, Addie said, "If you elect to become a nurse, you will graduate by the time we open our hospital. Now one last thing. If you cannot decide whether nursing is for you. Then, when the hospital opens, apply for the job of Nurse's Aide. The pay will be $750 a year (BW $28.85) with on-the-job training. Working as an aide will tell you whether nursing is for you. Within a year of being a Nurse's Aide, were you to apply and be accepted into nursing school, we will offer you the same special benefits and basically pay for your training with the same conditions of employment."

"In closing, please take an application to the nursing school. Even if you are uncertain, you will have it if you need it. For those of you who have specific and private questions, please see Addie before you leave. Last of all, if you apply and are accepted, notify us of your plans so we can arrange payment of your registration and admission fees. Thank you for your consideration."

*

That evening, the Trio arrived from Dallas. Having had supper on the train, the Trio were taken to their hotel for a night of rest. By morning, the Quad met in the hotel's restaurant for a full breakfast. The discussions were brisk and centered on the hospital. It was Sally Green who had the most revealing question as she asked, "if you are building a 75-bed hospital with physicians' offices and with currently only one practicing doc in town, where do you propose to get the help a community of 5,000 people will demand?"

Brad took his time to choose his words. "Well Sally it is not really a 'rocket science.' We are surrounded by medical people in training. Since we have 18 months left, Addie and I will start passing the word around that we need every specialty from Internal Medicine to Pathology, Surgery, and Obstetrics. Plus if we add that we will guarantee every medical staff a minimum yearly salary, then I am certain that we will get all the help we'll need and that includes all the nurses, heh?" "It was Ingrid who added, "really, you have the finances to add such guarantees?" "Yes we do!"

Cindy stayed on the same subject and asked, "I can see how doctor's income can be accounted for since they usually charge or bill the patients for services, but how do nurses get paid since they do not charge the patients directly for services?" "A few days ago I asked that same question to the CFO (chief financial officer) of Dallas General. The way he explained it is that the hospital bill has built-in the estimated costs of nursing care from nurse's aides, to ward nurses, to specialized nurses such as OR nurses, nurse anesthetics, and labor/delivery/nursery nurses. The nurses that assist surgeons are usually paid by the surgeon. So let us take an OR nurse as an example. We guarantee this nurse a yearly salary of $1,750. To reach that income her biweekly paycheck should be $67.31. If that income level was negotiated when the nurse was hired, we as the hospital owners need not add any money. If the biweekly pay does not reach $67.31 we will make up the difference either biweekly or quarterly, or even at the end-of-year." Cindy was surprised, "really, that is amazing." "Yes, this system is a national one and we plan to follow it!"

Tom was interested in how Doctors income would be tabulated. Brad said, "we will have several levels of care and income for MDs. The Internal Medicine MD will be guaranteed $3,000 per year (BW $115.38), the Pathologist/lab technician/phlebotomist gets $3,500 (BW $134.62), and the Surgeon/Obstetrician gets $4,000 (BW $153.85). But each doctor is responsible for paying his own office nurse. As a benefit for doctors, their all-expense housing in a new home on Doctor's Row will be included for the first year and a negotiable rate for future years. Plus let's not forget that all hospital employees, doctors, and their office nurse get free medical/maternity care and medical/injury full pay disability till their return to work."

Stanley added, "as any obstetrician, it may take many months to have his own income. Will you subsidize his biweekly income till he starts getting money for services?" "Absolutely and we will settle at the end of the year as we will guarantee his yearly income of $4,000."

Tom had an interesting point. "My reading indicates that Texas currently has 175 doctors per 100,000 population. That converts to +- 8 doctors for a community of 5,000 people as Amarillo's population is predicted to hit 5,000 by 1905 when your hospital will open. How many docs are you planning to start with?" "As a startup practice when patient visits and hospitalized patients take time to accumulate; we are planning to start with the local doc, Doctor Morse, and docs in: one in Internal Medicine, one in Obstetrics, one in Pathology/lab tech/phlebotomist, and two in General Surgery. When the need increases, we will

advertise in training centers and hope for the best."
Eyebrows were going up.

With the discussion having come to an end,
Addie said, "shall we take a 5-minute walk to the
construction site. When we were here at Thanksgiving,
our carpenter was planning to finish the inside walls
with wood after adding insulation. Who knows, that
may have changed." While walking Addie whispered
to Brad, "so if I am your office nurse and your
assistant at surgery, you will be the one to pay my
wages." Technically true, but if I give you a dollar out
of my income, it is the same as me keeping my entire
fees, heh?" "True, so how do I get paid?" "Trust me,
I know how to take care of you. You know, that before
morning you will be content, and be purring like a
kitten, heh?" "Yeah, been there, and know all about
that."

Once at the construction site, the guests were
amazed at the brick building before them—and with
five wings extending from the central connecting
'square' with a separate entrance to the Emergency
Ward. Entering they saw the central square with bare

brick walls. Greeted by the head contractor, Mike said, "you recalled that I had hired three subcontractors in electrical, plumbing, and central heating. Well when they started they pointed out that they could not do their work till the partition wall framing was up for every room in the hospital. That was so, because they were building ceiling main lines built over the central hallways, and with side branches to each room—so they needed to see where each room was and what was needed for water, electricity, oxygen, and heating ductwork. So voila, walk around and see where all the rooms will be located, and read each placard to find what the room will be used for. After your tour, we will meet in the square where we will set up chairs and I will answer your questions."

Starting in the Emergency Ward it was an open ward with bays that had wall oxygen, electricity, wash basins, water supply and others. It was clear that there would be at least four curtained bays. There was a room labeled for doctors, nurses, and pharmacy. Two rooms were enclosed and clearly labeled major trauma or burns. There were areas marked as storage. The last was an enclosed room labeled waiting room.

Next was the medical ward. Each patient room was labeled one or two occupants to share a toilet and wash basin. There were fourteen of them and a ward labeled '5 patient ward.' One area was labeled as bathrooms for private tub or standing shower bathing. At the end of the wing was a pharmacy, respiratory therapy room, storage, a nurses' station, a nook for doctors to write in the charts, and one room labeled 'infectious diseases.' Brad noted, "maximum occupancy is 33 patients."

The surgical wing started with two operating rooms, a sterilizing room with a surgical tool washing sink, an anesthesia room, and an outpatient prep room. Tom and Sally clearly liked what they saw. Beyond that on the opposite side was a four-bed curtained recovery room with a nurses' station and a pharmacy. Then were fourteen patient rooms that could be single or double occupancy with the usual shared toilet and wash sink. At the far end of the wing was the usual nurses' station, pharmacy, storage, and doctors' nook. Brad noted, "that's and extra 28 patients."

Their third tour was the labor and delivery. There were two separate labor rooms for either single or double occupancy with a toilet for each room. There were also two delivery rooms with tables convertible for birthing or for emergency C-sections. Between each room was the surgical scrubbing sink. Other rooms included at least one nurses' station. Stan had spotted the most important room, the doctor's lounge and bed.

Outside labor and delivery was a double nursery with a surgical scrubbing sink. The unit also had six post-delivery beds that were single occupancy rooms for mothers to sleep and nurse. Although not appreciated by everyone, Addie noted that Stan and Cindy were clearly pleased with that department. Brad noted an extra +- 10 patients.

Next was touring the 'square.' First was a fracture room and a side entrance to the Emergency Ward, an Xray room, and a large lab to include an office for the Pathologist/lab technician, and a room for outpatient phlebotomy. The most impressive spot in the 'square' was the volunteer counter where patients were directed to their destination.

The tour then entered the next wing. On the left was a huge kitchen and opposite the kitchen was a large room labeled dining room. Walking beyond that point was a room labeled laundry room and one labeled surgical gown sterilizing. For future use were four unclaimed rooms.

Stepping back in the square was the entrance to the last wing. The doctors and other offices with a waiting room in the 'square.' Walking down were doctor's offices and a separate treatment room with a toilet and sink. There were eight such offices for doctors—five for now and three for future needs. There were four other rooms with placards that read, combined accounting and purchasing, nursing supervisors, administrators/owners, and one left unclaimed. The Duo noted every face had a smile to share.

Sitting down with Mike the first question was from Daniel. "This is a nicely set up 71 bed hospital with a nursery. What happens if the future brings growth?" Mike smiled and said, "unless you missed it, each wing finishes at the end of the central passageway. At the end, the wall can be torn down and the wing extended as is needed. Personally, knowing what the population growth is expected, we will be back to extend wings." After a few more questions, the group made it clear that they had more questions for Brad and Addie, but would wait for a more private time.

*

The afternoon was left open as private time for each to enjoy.

Supper was a social event in the hotel's restaurant. Doctor Morse and Missus were invited. After extensive introductions, everyone had either a beer or wine to loosen their tongue. The questions were directed to Doctor Morse who said, "when I opened my office it was the old way with blood letting and homemade 'hocus pocus' remedies. I quickly abandoned bloodletting and started to use modern medicines as they came on the market. Today I use everything available but I assure you that it has been a challenge to stay up on new medicines or methods. Now at the age of 52 it is time for me to stop delivering babies. It has been demoralizing to lose a new mother to post-delivery hemorrhaging from a flaccid uterus or to have a stillborn. Today I know that a drug can be used to firm a delivery uterus as there are surgeons to do emergency C-sections or an emergency hysterectomy. To be clear, I cannot wait for an Obstetrician and Surgeons to rely on." Doctor Morse then got specific and verified what each doctor was training for; as Brad added that a doctor of Internal Medicine would be added. After the meal, when Doctor Morse departed, he had a smile from ear to ear.

Afterwards Addie announced, "tomorrow is Xmas day. We have church services at 9AM in the Methodist Church next to this hotel, for anyone who wish to attend, and afterwards, we have reserved a private dining room in this restaurant for the day. We will have liquid refreshments and a classic turkey dinner followed by an informative meeting. See you tomorrow."

That night, while in the hot tub, the Duo was having their first official business meeting. Addie started, "it seems to me that our friends seem interested in our hospital." "I may be wrong, but I think they are also interested in us and our need for doctors and specialized nurses. Don't you think so?" "Yes I do but the question really is whether it is as friends or as potential coworkers?" "Let's separate the two. Friends are forever and it doesn't matter whether we work together or work in separate communities— although the enjoyment is greater if we work together. There is no doubt that it is just as easy to work with friends as it is to work with strangers." "Ok, that is like saying that it is just as easy to fall in love with a rich person as a poor one, heh?" "Correct!"

"Now that we settled that, answer this!" Brad expected a tough question. "Is it appropriate or wise to bring six people into a business arrangement when we are just beginning our 5th month of a 24-month training program?" "Well at least we are thinking on the same wavelength. A premature 18-month business deal is like a marriage union. When I married you it was for love and I promised to care for you forever. I could never in my heart allow another woman to come between us."

Addie paused and then said, "so if a couple puts a high value on their word, and they commit to asking us to reserve a medical position, and if we accept them, then when asked about that position all we can say is that the position has been filled, heh?" "Correct!" "So do we insist on signed contracts with them?" "Yes and no. If something happens in the next 20 months and a couple wishes out of the arrangement, well we have no choice since we don't want coworkers that don't want to be with us. Actually WE need to give each couple a written guarantee that we will keep the requested position available no matter what other medical staff request—even if abilities are not equal."

Addie then added, "you know how women like to talk in secrecy; well the talk has been on safe sex and the wish for us gals to never separate. So, unless I did not align my stars correctly, tomorrow we will be adding six essential coworkers to our medical staff." "Yes, that is a big step. So six down and many more to go!" "Really, who are the others we need?" "I have recently observed the wards and have come down to this list:

1. Internal Medicine MD
2. One more nurse anesthetist.
3. Two more OR nurses.
4. An OR supervisor.
5. A nursing supervisor.
6. An accountant.
7. A purchasing agent."

Addie added, "let's not forget we also need at least +-25 ward nurses." "I know and hopefully they won't all be high maintenance like my loving wife!" "I'll remind you that I only ask one thing of you!" "Yes I know dear, and with all this talk, I am getting way behind."

*

It was Xmas morning and the Duo was up early. Neither would admit it, but both were anxious over how the day would progress. After several coffees, the

Duo got together and prepared a business contract that guaranteed their position would be available on their graduation day some +-18 months later. Each couple had the duties listed of each applicant as well as their guaranteed first year income. The contract was to be signed by two witnesses. Abbie went ahead and typed all three contracts with the names of each couple.

The Duo arrived at church a bit late, but as they walked in, saw the other three couples already sitting in their pews. The minister was hot under the collar as the spoke on 'commitment.' Although he was talking about committing to the church and Jesus Christ on the day of his birth, everyone had the word in their thoughts—and it wasn't about the minister's trend of thought.

After the service, the Quad made their way to their hotel and by 10:30 were all holding a cold beer or a glass of white wine. All were tense as the alcohol slowly dulled the senses and led to smiles and laughter. By noon, the group was invited to the table as their meal was brought in and served family style. With everyone served, Brad asked Addie to say grace. A bit surprised, she managed to find some poignant words.

Lord thank you for the food we are about to enjoy. Especially we give thanks for, the training we are about to continue, and we ask that you keep us eight friends together for years to come. Amen.

Everyone delved into their meal, but not one could get Addie's words out of their heads. It was a slow dragged-out meal with seconds followed by coffee and the choice of custard or sugar pie with ice cream. With the table cleared and fresh coffee served, a silence took over the party room. Finally Brad stood and said, "a difficult time is upon us and it is time for you all to speak your mind on what we plan to build in this community."

There was a silence in the room that seemed would never end. Finally Daniel stood and said, "I have been chosen to speak on behalf of the other five 'chickens.'" Silence persisted. "To cut to the chase, we have all enjoyed the tour, love your design of the hospital, doctor's offices, Doctor's Row, and highly respect your financial offer to say the least of your benefits and housing. There is not much more to say, except that all six of us would ask that you consider hiring us to fill six essential positions—as premature as some might say. So for your consideration each of us has prepared a short statement that applies individually to each of us. Tom will start."

TOM. "I want to make it clear, that even if I have an MD degree in Internal Medicine, I plan to practice my life's dream of being a surgeon. I will use my medical knowledge to help care for my post-op patients but not to practice Internal Medicine. Now I am totally enthused with the hospital's layout especially the operating area next to the recovery room and the surgical ward. Even so, you have a perfect layout of doctor's offices with each a treatment room for minor surgery. All in all, I could not ask for more. I hope to be busy so I don't need to take your payroll guarantee. You have handed me a perfect practice location and coworkers on a golden platter. I accept and thank you."

SALLY. "Tom and I have for years wondered what it would be like to leave our training security and go off in the world to practice surgery. We can all agree that could be an anxiety producing situation. Well now planning to come back to Amarillo to join this medical group/hospital has become a 'piece of cake.' I personally look forward to being Tom's surgical assistant even if he doesn't give me a paycheck—for I have my own bank book, heh? Let's not forget the luxury of living in a brand-new house next to the hospital. We hope you accept our request for a spot in your medical dream?"

DANIEL. "In my position as Pathologist, I would be a hospital employee but I would like to clarify my duties. As Pathologist, I would be responsible to prepare tissue samples for histology analysis, blood chemistry analysis, peripheral blood smear exam, blood hemoglobin/hematocrits, outpatient phlebotomy, IV cannulation for IV fluids and blood transfusion. When the EKG machines become available I will add those to my duties and provide a reading for all with its clinical significance. Blood typing of all surgical and

OB patients will be my responsibility. As a certified anesthetist, I will serve as a backup anesthetist in an emergency, but not as a regular worker in the OR. Coming soon is blood type specific 'compatibility' to add another level for transfusion safety. And last, for me to have a guaranteed income and free housing in a 'state of the art hospital' is a dream come true. Thanks."

INGRID. "I have little to say. If my husband is happy, I am happy. Other than that, there is no doubt it will be a pleasure to provide anesthesia for you, Tom and Stan. Night call for emergencies is not a problem especially if I can share nights with another anesthetist and I can walk to the hospital from Doctor's Row. As a hospital employee I will be getting a hospital paycheck but your guarantee is a security backup. Just to add, I will be watching your surgical technique to help judge the level of anesthesia you require. I am all in. This is a great deal for both of us."

STANLEY. "In my life I would never have imagined so much handed to me. Housing, guaranteed income, a state-of-the-art labor and delivery area in a new hospital. It will make the long training worthwhile. My goal is to learn the proper technique in forceps deliveries and be an expert in performing C-Sections. I have no urge to do routine abdominal-gynecological surgery as that belongs in the realm of general surgery. In the same light, I would rely on you and Tom to assist me to do emergency hysterectomies for post-delivery hemorrhaging that does not respond to ergot alkaloids or external stimulation. I will do my own D&Cs after a miscarriage. Looking back, it was nice to hear that Doctor Morse would stop performing deliveries which will be a godsend for me in establishing my practice. Last of all, I will not be performing abortions. Thank you for the housing benefit and the guaranteed income."

CINDY. "Well last but not least, heh? It is clear that as Stan's office nurse I will be without a paycheck, so to speak. But when I work in labor and delivery, are my services part of the hospital bill, or are they as part of Stan's delivery fee?" Addie jumped in, "yet to be determined but you will not lose out!" "Then I am so happy to be returning to this community and this brand-new hospital, working with currently trained staff with a liberal approach to life and work—and out of the dark ages of medicine. Thank you for the benefits and for considering us."

There was a long pause as Addie said, "those were encouraging words. Anyways Brad will sum this up!" "We are proud to say that we would be happy to hire all of you—just like a long engagement between fiancés." Daniel added, we are all ready to sign a contract if you have one ready." Brad looked at the group and said, "all Addie and I need from you all is a handshake or a hug. We will give you a contract that guarantees your position in +- 18 months. The men stepped up and provided such as the gals hugged everybody. Unbeknownst to the men were the gals whispering, *"we did it guys, we'll be together forever. Thank God the men saw the right path to follow. Shush is the word, heh?"*

That is when Addie brings out three contracts. Having each contract signed by two random witnesses, the Duo signed the contracts and handed each one to the appropriate couple. "Read this carefully and you do not sign it, it is a promise from Addie and me that your position will be available in +-18 months from today. It is a security that we will not abandon you and never leave you in a lurch."

After a pause, Brad said, "there is one more bit of business to cover. As new workers, you are all eligible for a 'sign on' bonus. Realistically, we are sure you are getting low in funds after years of training. We know your registration is paid for, but spending money will soon be getting low. So we have computed that for the next 18 months we are giving you a monthly stipend to cover personals, coffee, snacks, underwear, or whatever you need." Addie finishes to write three bank drafts and hands them to Brad. "We hope $40 a month will be enough and maybe a bit left over for you to move after graduation." Each couple was handed a $720 bank draft. The comments were enlightening, "oh great, I can buy sanitary napkins again, unlimited coffee for the next 18 months, and finally new underwear. Sally had the best comment, she started crying, hugged Addie and just said, "thank you, love you so ... heh?"

Once things cooled down, Brad asked, "would you all take a moment to write down what you want in the departments that affect each of you, Now is the time to change construction things before things are etched in stone. Plus make a list of things you will need. As examples, Stan you will need a group of specific delivery forceps and more, Daniel you will need a microtome to prepare histology slides and several reagents to do chemistry analysis, and Tom you will need certain tools to do outpatient surgery and so on. Addie and I have already prepared our lists and we'll bring all the lists to Mike tomorrow."

Addie then said, "in closing pass the word around that we are looking for an Internist, another nurse anesthetist, two OR nurses, an OR supervisor, a Nursing Supervisor, an accountant, a purchasing agent, and about 25 ward nurses. See you all back at Dallas General Hospital, heh?"

CHAPTER 6

The Training Hoops

Addie moved right in the operating room scene. First she learned how to sterilize surgical equipment by using the steam sterilizer as well as the dry heat technique. Then came sterilizing OR gowns, drapes, and sheets with the dry heating technique. Secondly she learned how to stack each tool and its duplicates correctly in the surgical kits as well as learn the proper name of each tool. Some of those things she had already learned at home from Brad but never let on that she knew more than she would admit. It took two weeks before Addie was allowed to become the second OR nurse during an actual operation—that was an observing OR nurse in training.

That evening Brad explained how the training 'system' worked. "Recently I had a chat with our OR supervisor as she explained how the 'system' worked. Over the next weeks, you will have more and more responsibility added and by, say a month, you will be assigned your first operation as you being the only OR nurse. As you know, everyone has a different learning curve so each student takes his or her own time to be fully certified—and that goes for doctors as Resident 2 to become an attending." "Ok, but you know that I am impatient and I want to zip over an OR nurse's training and start my last stage as a surgeon's assistant."

There was a pause as Brad said, "in that light, let me teach you a skill that will quickly advance you as an OR nurse and then we'll talk about the training involved to become a nurse surgical assistant" "Ok!" "An OR nurse who gingerly hands a surgeon a new tool will require the surgeon to lift his eyes off the field of view to see where the requested instrument is. That is a no-no! Snap your wrist like so … and be assertive so the surgeon knows he was handed his requested instrument. Start using it now and you'll be surprised the eyebrows you'll see lifted over their facemasks. Now let's practice both the right- and left-hand toss."

When she mastered the handout, Brad said, "now let's talk about training for a surgeon's assistant position. Remember I told you that you would only be my assistant once I became an attending?" "Yes, I remember that." "What I did not mention is that while you are training for either the OR nurse or the assistant surgeon's position, I will never be scheduled to be either the primary surgeon or the assistant surgeon. Training of a wife is done thru the system and a husband-and-wife team is usually not allowed till I am a full attending and you certified as a surgeon's assistant."

Addie was stunned, "So the only time I'll see you at work is the occasional lunch together or when we come home at night?" "Yes, that is another sacrifice we must make to get this rare training." "Well if it has to be, we will MANAGE, heh?"

Over two weeks, she used the 'snap' technique 100% of the time. One day, the OR supervisor, Missus

Fogarty, came to Addie who was preparing the instruments for a hysterectomy. "Missus Kelly, I have had several requests from some superior surgeons that you be assigned to them even if your husband is the assigned assistant surgeon. So starting this morning, this is your first case as the assigned 1st OR nurse. Good luck and don't let me down, heh?"

As the surgeons were scrubbing. The attending, Doctor Willis, said, "you have been assisting me several times in the past weeks and it is clear to me that you know what you are doing. So let's hope this is an easy procedure, heh?" Walking in the operating room, Addie was the OR nurse who had to gown and glove both doctors. Brad had a smile from ear to ear but Addie had a stone face. Suddenly, nurse supervisor Fogarty announced, "today doctors, we have a new top of the line OR nurse. Missus Kelly."

The surgeons were ready as Doctor Willis snapped his glove and the surgery started. Addie handed Doc Willis a #10 blade by the handle as the blade was then transferred to Brad. "Are you ready Doctor?" "Yes Doctor." "Then proceed and I will be your assistant."

Brad made the skin incision and the bleeders were everywhere. Addie was snapping one hemostat after another—snap, snap, snap … as Brad was trying hard to hide his smile.

The operation went smoothly as Addie was following the procedure and managed to have ¾ of the instruments ready before asked. As Brad was closing, Doc Willis said, "now provide an incisional suture that will hide the incision. Brad was about to ask for the proper suture as Addie handed him a 3-0 chromic catgut. "Suture free Doctor, heh?" After the operation, Doc Willis added, "that was a perfect operation Doctor Kelly. We'll meet in the doctor's lounge and I will be honored to certify you for a hysterectomy. And thank you Missus Kelly, nice job as usual—wait a minute." Looking back and forth he asked, "are you two related or something?"

After a short pause, Brad said, "yes Doc, Adelle or Missus Kelly is my wife!" "Well blow me over—ha-ha-ha-haah. Missus Fogarty, I think you should certify the Missus as well, heh?" "Already have doctor!" After shedding the surgical garb, Brad came over and gave

Addie a kiss even if supervisor Fogarty and the nurse anesthetist were still with the patient. Brad then whispered, 'seven down and five to go!'"

*

Weeks had gone by and Addie always managed to be home by 5:30 but Brad was getting home later and later. Tonight it was 9PM when a tired Brad appeared at their apartment. Addie did not want to complain but asked why he was now working from 6AM to 9PM. "Well it is the result of the fact that I am assisting at least three major operations each day but that includes doing the 'History and Physical,' checking labs, examining the patient, and writing the chart up on all three patients. Plus after the operation the assistant surgeon is in charge of the patient while in the recovery room. Assuming that recovery patients are observed for an average of three hours, when the third case finishes at 5 or 6PM, well I cannot discharge the recovery room patient to the surgical ward until the appropriate time has passed and the patient is ready for ward care."

Addie paused and then asked, " maybe you should do two cases a day like most 2nd year residents are doing?" "I considered that, but with 9 down and three to go, and with a wife nursing assistant surgeon soon to be certified—well I need to be ready for you, heh?" Addie backed down, reheated his supper and prepared his hot bath. Once in bed, Brad fell asleep so quickly that nothing conjugal ever happened.

The next month had several events that were marked by changes. Addie was allowed to prematurely enter the surgical assistant program for nurses. Brad had an event that tried his leadership. Brad was checking on his third patient of the day when a panicking recovery nurse and the OR supervisor asked Brad to get involved with a left chest tube patient who was having a low blood pressure and a fast pulse. Brad checked the situation and recognized 'blood loss shock.' He ordered an emergency chest and KUB (abdominal) Xray. There in front of their eyes was the problem. The chest tube had gone down thru the diaphragm into the spleen instead of upwards toward the lung apex.

Brad first asked, "has this patient's doctor been contacted?" "Not available despite we had told him of the low blood pressure." "Well what had he said, "his exact words were, 'well if you had a chest tube in you, you would also have a low blood pressure' as he walked away." Brad only response was get me Doctor Tom Hall as an assistant, notify the surgical board's, Doctor Huxley, of the situation, and notify the OR that we are doing a lifesaving emergency splenectomy—STAT!"

Doctor Kelly made one deft incision, entered the bloody abdominal cavity, and applied a Kelly forceps to the splenic artery/vein trunk. Just then, Doctor Huxley was heard saying, "hello doctors, I hear you need an attending to do a splenectomy, heh? Well I see you have things under control. I have seen the alarming X rays and agree with your diagnosis."

The surgeons finished doing the splenectomy and then Tom reinserted the chest tube upwards to the chest apex as Brad sutured the hole in the diaphragm. Attaching the tube to an air trapping system for a pneumothorax, Tom returned to the abdominal site to help Brad empty the abdomen of several units of blood. As the surgeons were closing up, a blood transfusion was started after a total of three liters of saline had been infused to keep up a lifesaving blood pressure.

Doctor Huxley finally said, "that was quite an impressive procedure, let's meet in the doctor's lounge where I will certify both of you for a splenectomy and a thoracostomy tube—a job well done." After the signing Doctor Crump arrived in a huff. "What is the meaning of all this and how could you allow two residents to do such a drastic procedure. I will file a complaint of interference against you!"

"That does it you flaming idiot. Look at these X rays." "I don't use ghost pictures they mean nothing to me." "Yes we know from past experiences, well let me explain. This is your chest tube in the bottom of the chest. It turns downward thru the diaphragm and then right into the spleen. On top of it all, the recovery nurse tried to tell you something was wrong but you just ignored her as a dumb nurse. You are lucky these doctors saved your patient otherwise we would be referring you for malpractice leading to a patient's death. Well as of this moment, you no longer have admitting privileges in this hospital and I will file an emergency complaint with the board of medical practice. You will lose your medical/surgical license for all of Texas because you are a quack." As the docs left, Brad said, "11 down and one to go" as Tom said, "7 down and five to go!"

It was two weeks later that Brad and Tom were both working in the Emergency Ward when a middle-aged man appeared with abdominal pain and a fever. Brad got the case as next in line. The first surprise was that it was LLQ (left lower quadrant) pain and not RLQ pain of appendicitis. The lab showed a high white cell count high in neutrophils (signs of a bacterial infection). Brad had Tom check the patient as a potential assistant surgeon when the attending surgeon assigned to the Emergency Ward arrived. Doctor Colon said, "well Doctor Kelly and Hall, it seems we have had several cases together lately, so what have we here."

The doctors shared the history and when asked what their tentative diagnosis was, Brad said, "in view of the patient's age, his history of eating canned whole kernel corn regularly, and the location of pain; we believe he has acute diverticulitis or a diverticulitis/abscess." "Very good, then I shall schedule an exploratory laparotomy for this afternoon and both of you should assist."

With the slap of the gloves, Doc Colon stood back, positioned Brad across Tom, had the OR nurse hand the #10 blade to Brad and said, "I have seen you both at work during other cases and I believe you are ready. Proceed Doctor Kelly and use Doctor Hall as your assistant. I am an observer, but an easily critical one, heh."

The abdominal cavity was entered and a transverse colon abscess was identified. Doubly clamping above and below the abscess, the diseased colon was resected. The two surgeons were moving along performing an anastomosis using 2-0 cotton. Brad did the posterior portion as Tom sutured the front portion. When done, Doctor Colon examined their work and said, "that ladies and gentlemen is a perfect anastomosis—as good as I could have done. Very good doctors, are you done?" Brad gave Tom the nod who added, "no doctor, we need to close the abdominal wall and need to bring a loop of proximal colon to the skin to divert its contents for 4-6 weeks—a temporary diverting colostomy."

Doctor Colon looked at the OR nurse and said, "please hand Doctor Hall a #10 blade!" The colostomy was done as Doctor Colon invited the surgeons to the doctor's lounge. In front of other attendings, Doctor Colon proudly said, "that was a perfect operation. Here are four documents. I am certifying you on both procedures, bowel resection and colostomy. Congratulations," as other attendings joined in with the applause. On their way-out Brad said, "13 down and 0 to go, as Tom added, 9 down and 3 to go!"

The word got around the hospital that Doctor Kelly had met the requirement of 12 certified major operations done in this hospital. When Brad got home late as usual, Addie jumped in his arms as Brad entered their home. Addie wouldn't let go as the Duo celebrated their fortune.

Two days later the Duo was called to Doctor Huxley's office. "Well here we are, it is the first of June and you still have 16 months to go in your training. To start with, here are two forms. The first is for Addie, it seems that nurse Fogarty has certified you as a surgeon's assistant." Addie was totally surprised but proud to be done with her training stages. Brad was also assigned his 'attending certification.' Doctor Huxley then handed them their new ID badges— Bradley Kelly MD, surgical attending and Adelle Kelly RN, surgical assistant.

"As it is customary, you are both on a week's vacation as I know you will be heading to Amarillo to see how your hospital is coming along, heh? Doctor Kelly, upon your return, you will be assigned to the Emergency Ward and Trauma Room where you will gather your own surgical cases since you do not have a local practice to feed you the cases. Trust me, you will end up with more cases than you ever expected. Get some R & R before your return, heh? As far as you Addie, you are free to come and go as long as you are available when Brad schedules an emergency or elective procedure. Unless I am mistaken, you will be involved with several projects that affect your hospital's readiness—see you in a week, heh?"

*

The Duo took the 9AM train to Amarillo and arrived at 6PM. After unpacking, they walked down to the hotel's restaurant. Waiting for their fried chicken order, Addie said, "don't you think it is time to start advertising for the medical doctor, nurse anesthetist, two OR nurses, and ancillary help." "Well we know we need all of them, but who is on the ancillary list?" "That would include: an accountant, a purchasing agent, an OR supervisor, a nursing supervisor, a pharmacist, and an Xray technician." "What about a laundry worker, a housekeeping person or service, a cook, and nurses' aides?" "Now the original group has to come from a training center or big city hospital. But ancillary help has to come from town as we are an equal opportunity employer." "Ok, I see the difference." "We can wait for the ancillary help till we are close to opening but now is the time to hire the professionals. So, I will send a telegram to Sally and ask her to post the positions in the residents, nursing, technician, and the business lounges of our training center."

After a blissful night and replenishing breakfast, the Duo stopped at the telegraph office to send the telegram to Sally and ask her to post the listings today. Afterwards, they walked into the hospital. Mike greeted them and said, "didn't expect you but so glad you are here. Let me show you what and where we are up to. Deciding to finish each wing in a clockwise fashion we started with the physician's wing—also on that wing since Doc Morse wants to move in sooner than later. Anyways, you can see that the ceiling over the central archway is full of water mains, electrical mains, heating ductwork, and the forgotten telephone line. Then the utilities branched out to each room and the walls were finished once the end utility adapters were ready for covering. These rooms are ready except for furniture, the water closet, and wash sink. So on the left side we have rooms for accountant, purchasing agent, nursing supervisor, and administrator's office and one extra unassigned room. There is a candlestick handheld phone in all the administrative offices and in a soundproof room in the doctors' wing for all docs to use. In all we ended up with eight private doctor offices each with a treatment room."

The Duo walked around and was pleased with the layout. "So which wing are you finishing next?" "Well all my carpenters and the subcontractors want the kitchen wing next. They are looking forward to a hot lunch. Once we start the wing, we will finish it before moving on. So we will finish the dining room, the laundry room, housekeeping, a men and ladies' bathroom, and the two empty rooms at the end." Addie added, "and keep those two rooms empty for now till we know their future use."

Brad was curious and asked, "it is nice to have a full commercial kitchen, but you need a cook to have prepared meals." "Ah yes, well I have a widowed aunt that is a well-known cook in town who has also taken courses on different meals like, low salt, low acid, low this and that. Plus she is willing to do her own grocery shopping." Addie smiled and said, "hire her, and give her a salary of $1,000 (twice minimum wages) a year with medical and disability benefits."

"Great, well there is another request. It is high time to have a purchasing agent on the site. I am sure you know the hundreds of items that a functioning hospital with private doctor's office can utilize. Not to criticize but you doctors and nurses take the items for granted. As an example, start making a list of the items needed in the wards, the offices, the OR, the cast room, and the lab. We will talk again tomorrow."

"Now for the last item, the bank real-estate agent has told me that the six-room apartment next door will be coming on the market within a week. Is this something that you would be interested in for essential workers?" Brad was surprised and got the nod from Addie. "Yes, what is the agent's name?" "Victor Horskins." "Ok, well we have two projects to work on so we will meet here tomorrow morning."

Victor was glad to discuss the apartment building. "It is only five years old, solid construction with a steel roof, three apartments on each floor, all units with two bedrooms—one as a bedroom the other as a nursery or office, or both. Cookstove and heating stoves are propane. Each apartment is fully furnished with very good stuff, and it has city water, sewage, electricity, and phone service There is one empty apartment and the other five have leases that expire within six to nine months. And all within a two-minute walk to your hospital. Shall we go check it out and see the empty apartment—as the other five have the same design and amenities." "Lead the way!"

The Duo was impressed and tried not to show it but Victor knew he had found a buyer and would be able to save on advertising and showing it to nosey people who did not have a pot to pee in—as the saying goes. After the detailed visit, the Duo and Victor were sitting in Wayne's Diner and enjoying a late morning bearpaw pastry and coffee. Eventually, Brad asked, "why is this place for sale, it looks like a nice business investment?" "The builder just passed away and the widow wants to liquidate the family assets. It is priced right in the middle of a low-high price range and will sell quickly once we put it on the market." "Is the deed clear?" "100% and the bank has power of attorney to accept or reject a bid, can issue a bill of sale, and authorize a new deed."

Addie could no longer wait, "how much does the widow want for a cash payment today." "Oh my, we never expected that, but the bank policy of purchases with cash instead of a bank loan is a 10% savings." Brad was even more impatient and said, "how much Victor, the lowest amount you will accept for cash?" Victor was thinking about not losing his selling fee and finally blurted out, "$6,000 or one thousand per apartment fully furnished. That is a steal and you know it" "Why?" "Well it is plain to see that the bank wants to support your philanthropy in building us a hospital." Addie got the nod when she said, "Sir, you have a deal. Let's go to the bank, pay for it, and sign the papers!"

*

The afternoon was spent making a list of items that would be needed to supply the new hospital. With their memory banks exhausted they had come down to four lists of necessary items which overlapped.

WARDS

Pharmacy meds, dressings, IV fluids and tubing, oxygen cannulas, bedpans, urinals, bedside commode, emesis basin, bed sheets, pillows, visitor chairs, toilet paper, waterproof bed pads, sanitary napkins, sitz baths, foley catheters to drainage, chest tube drainage and air trapping, and hypodermic needles.

FRACTURE ROOM

Extremity splints, plaster and protective padding, upper arm slings, saws and chisels, and wooden heels for walking casts.

OR

Carbolic acid, iodine, antiseptic creams, honey, surgical gowns, caps, face mask, gloves, patient drapes and sheets, chloroform, ether, Nitrous Oxide, 'coned facemasks' for anesthesia administration, and orthopedic kit of stainless-steel screws, plates, and tools.

GENERAL (INCLUDING OFFICE SUPPLIES)

Injectable meds, prescription blanks, dressing trays, pelvic speculums and anoscopes, skin biopsy tools, Unna boots, blood pressure cuffs, stethoscopes, fetoscopes and otoscopes.

At that point, the Duo realized that their list was not complete but did not know how to make it complete. As it was, they realized that when the hospital doors opened, they would realize what was missing—if not too late. Being stuck in limbo, the Duo went back to the hospital to give their list to Mike. As they walked in they saw a young man waiting at the information counter. Addie addressed him by saying, "we are the Kelly's and who might you be?" "I am JD Sinclair and I am a current graduate of the same training center as you."

"I am a trained purchasing agent. I am here in town because my parents live here as I was raised in town. I just got an emergency telegram from my college roommate telling me you have just posted your list of needed ancillary helpers. I wish to apply for a job." "Well let's have a chat." After 15 minutes, the Duo knew he was the man for the job. Then Addie pushed the issue. She handed him the list of items they had ordered months ago and the list they had prepared today. Showing both to JD, he tried to hide his astonishment. Finally he said, "here is the current list that our training center is using. It is ten pages long and has at least 250 items per page. As an example, you wrote dressings. Did you realize that there are 17 different types of dressings and sizes?"

The Duo was flabbergasted and JD noticed it. "What I suggest is that you take the ten pages, check off any item you want excluding those already ordered and we will meet tomorrow and get a final order prepared." Brad was taken back as he said, "why are you doing this for us, you don't know us from Adam and Eve?" "Because Amarillo will always be my home and you and your hospital will benefit my family."

Addie then shocked Brad and JD when she asked, "which job are you looking for?" "Why, it is the purchasing agent's job." "Well, why don't you come and work for us?" Brad jumped in and said, "we'll pay you the same wages as a specialized nurse--$1750 a year or biweekly $67.31 with medical and full disability till you return to work, and a free apartment next door for the first year." "Really, you are offering me this hospital's purchasing agent's job?" "Hell yes. As a matter of fact, walk with us to the physician's wing and we will show you your office?" Looking at an empty office, Addie said, "go to White's Office Supplies and order whatever you want for office furniture." Brad then said, "follow me to where you will have your central supply storage. They included Mike and walked to beyond the laundry room and said, "we need shelving everywhere for the hospital's central supply." "And JD, while at Whites, get signs made up for your office and the central supply two rooms."

The Duo then walked JD to the apartment complex. JD was more than elated at the luxury, so Brad asked, "when can you start?" "Today, I will go home and get my stuff, move in, and go buy some office furniture. Then we will meet in the AM to go over the items you chose off the master list."

The Duo could not believe that they had to choose items off a 2,500-r piece master list. Slowly they each independently reviewed the first page and checked off what was needed—after they had put their excuse for a tentative needed list aside. After the third page was done, they put the task aside and went to eat supper. Afterwards, they resumed their job. It was late when they finished the tenth page. Addie had added each page and came to a total of +-1,000 items— anywhere from one to ten of each.

The next morning, JD joined them for breakfast. Waiting for his order he perused the checked-off items. "This is perfect and will get your hospital and doctor's offices running the first day. Now the problem is that ¾ of these items come from the eastern manufacturers. That means we should order now to have things here by 16 months." "Fine put the orders in!" "Uh-uh, first time orders need to be paid by telegraph vouchers?" After breakfast, that led to a visit to the bank where JD was given withdrawal permission to pay for his telegraph vouchers as well as local purchases.

*

The Duo returned to Dallas to resume their training as Brad was an attending surgeon assigned to cover the EW and the Trauma Center. Addie was on call for any procedure Brad was scheduling. Early on Addie realized that it was too early to advertise the positions for their hospital, now that they had a purchasing agent, she added a placard that said "think about these coming positions and apply by next April. Addie agreed that she would do all the interviews and the hiring except for the Doctor of Internal Medicine—Brad agreed to be involved with that one.

It was a bad week for gunshots. There was a band of outlaws that had been marauding and shooting their victims. Brad and Addie were able to handle the abdominal gunshots that required manually running both the small and large intestines to look for bullet holes that needed to be sewn over as well as finding the bullet that needed to be pulled out to avoid infections. After careful surgery their survival rate was 80% if the large intestine full of bacteria was not seriously damaged or with much spill.

Chest gunshots were a new area of management. Fortunately the head of chest surgery was available as Brad and Tom were both heavily involved. Tom had just made attending but Sally was still an OR nurse as the four made a good chest team. The surgeons learned how to do lobe resections, over sew a bullet hole, how to stop bleeding with purse sutures, and how to extract a bullet from the lung. After any surgery the entrance thoracostomy was sutured closed as a chest tube to drainage and air trapping was left in place till air and fluid was no longer present.

The surgeons also had medically ill patients requiring surgery as trauma would lacerate tender organs such as liver and spleen. The most common operations were appendectomy and bleeding ulcers but the entire gamut of some 20 procedures were regularly done. Eventually Sally was certified as assistant surgeon and the two teams were a regular name on the surgical board—usually as an emergency.

Brad and Tom were the two EW attendings and they shared night call. It was a busy night when Stan came to the EW looking for the attending surgeon. Stan came to Brad's bedroom and asked him to help him perform an emergency C-Section for a case of sudden fetal distress.

Stan had done plenty of C-Sections with other attendings but had not yet been certified. Brad was up like a bullet as the two surgeons headed to the OR.

Stan snapped his gloves after the mom was prepped and draped.. At full speed, Stan made a bladder flap, cut into the uterus, and extracted the baby with three loops of umbilical cord around the baby's neck. While Stan was resuscitating the baby, Brad extracted the placenta, injected the ergot alkaloid, and started closing the uterus. Then Stan closed the abdominal incision. After the procedure was completed, with both mom and baby doing well, Brad shocked Stan. "Here is your certification for a C-Section. It is my pleasure to sponsor my first 10/10 certification for a job very well done; congratulations my friend."

It was now August 15, 1904, and the Duo took a few days off to check out the hospital's progress. At their first meeting with Mike, the high school principal walked in and handed the Duo a pile of application acceptances. The principal said, "17 graduates applied to that nursing school last winter and all were accepted into the Kelly program. When you return, Doctor Huxley will need a bank draft for $17,000. Thank You."

The tour included the finding of a rectangular hole in the brick wall of both operating rooms and the recovery room. Brad asked what those boarded up areas were for. Mike said, "look at the ceiling and you will see several extra electrical wires in one pipe. These are for high voltage room air conditioners. It is possible, according to Leonard Plumbing, that within a year, new hospitals will be able to get a limited supply of room air conditioners without retrofitting them. If it doesn't happen then it will happen sometime in the future and we will be set up to connect them, heh?"

The rest of the tour was controlled by JD Sinclair. JD pointed out that several rooms were nearly done and it was time to make them 'operationally ready.' "These rooms included: Pathology and laboratory, doctor's offices, operating rooms and recovery, labor and delivery, nursery, maternity wards—all in that sequential order. Doctor Morse agreed to get the fracture and dental rooms ready—of course, after his office and treatment room were done, heh?"

JD added that the supplies for these rooms were still arriving and starting on December 1st with Doctor Greene, he would spend a week helping the doctor get organized. Then each week a new department head should arrive to spend their week of organization. To Addie, she knew she had to hire an OR supervisor and a general nursing supervisor, as she herself would organize the doctors' offices/treatment rooms. The rest of the departments would be done by the original three doctors. Doctor Hall would work with the new OR supervisor to get their important operating theater properly organized.

After the hospital tour was done, Mike admitted that the hospital would be done no later than April 1st, 1905. The Duo then toured the Doctor's Row. The Duo's house would be done and ready to move in by Thanksgiving as the other four would at least be secured for the winter.

When the Duo returned to Dallas, Addie started aggressively looking for the OR supervisor and the nursing supervisor. It took almost a month as both positions were filled. The remainder of the ancillary workers (accountant, OR nurses and X Ray tech) would be filled in March as all new workers received a $250 sign-on bonus. Also of note, the new workers would all end up in the new apartment—OR super, nursing super, X Ray tech, accountant, two OR nurses as roommates, and the preexisting purchasing agent.

It was an important day the week before Xmas when a medical student scheduled for graduation in May, requested an appointment. Winston and

Marlene Reinhart were applying for the medical doctor and nurse anesthetist positions. Present at the meeting were The Duo and Ingrid Greene as current nurse anesthetist. The meeting was congenial and the Duo and Ingrid fell in love with the husband-and-wife team. Winston's selling point other than his personality was that he would add an 'informed doctor' regarding currently used new medicines and the ones soon to come on the market. Marlene, with two years' experience, would be glad to share the evening on call schedule with Ingrid. Both were hired before they knew they would be living in a new house on Doctor's Row; free of charge for one year. When told of their guaranteed salaries and doctor's office, both admitted they had no idea of their salary or benefits. Their sign-on bonus of $500, was even a greater shock, and graciously accepted as needed funds.

The fall of 1904 was a busy time for Brad and Tom. They managed to perform at least three major cases each day. Addie and Sally were now full-time surgical assistants as the two surgeons would manage to do the surgery or stand by to observe and share the experience. Looking back at their schedule of performed surgery to Xmas showed:

1. Infections of appendix, gall bladder, and colon diverticulum.
2. Life threatening hemorrhaging as in peptic ulcers, colon bleeds, uterine hemorrhages, and gunshots.
3. Trauma to abdomen, chest, extremities as well as the many fractures.

When December arrived, department heads were spending their weeks setting up their part of the Kelly Memorial Hospital. Despite their heavy schedules, the entire Kelly group managed to hear Daniel present the lecture on EKG's as they all realized that this tool would soon be available. Along with all their training, everyone took the tours thru the Cancer Center Radiation Department. This was important since the surgeons would do a laparotomy to resect a tumor, and if not resectable, would have to send their patient to Dallas General for radiation treatments.

By Xmas, the Duo was planning to do their last trip to Amarillo. Their house would be done and complete meals could be enjoyed in the hospital cafeteria. The Duo did not have changes to make and were reassured that all doctors' homes and the hospital would be completed by April 1st. With that reassurance, the Duo returned to Dallas to celebrate the holidays with their friends and new workers. After the holidays would be the last months of their training but no one realized that it could be shorter than expected.

CHAPTER 7

Preparing for a Hospital Practice

Upon arrival in Dallas, the Duo reserved a private dining room at Georgiana's Diner; a private location outside of the hospital setting but within walking distance to the hospital. The group of five doctors, their wives, and all the new workers already hired gathered at 10AM for liquid refreshments. Although everyone in the room had received their sign-on bonuses, the Duo managed to add a $50 bank draft to every couple's Xmas card, or $25 to each single new worker. By noon, the classic turkey dinner with all the fixings was served family style. With plenty of coffee and seconds on the many desserts, the Kelly group was totally satiated.

At the end of dinner, Brad announced, "well here we go. This is our last jaunt. The question is whether we have eight months to graduation or whether we all qualify for early certification. Whatever happens, we need to stay till we get our certifications." With a unanimous agreement, the celebration ended and all returned to their housing.

The winter became monotonous for the surgeons. They were operating on the standard 20 procedures from day to day. Both Brad and Tom admitted that they were confident in their abilities to do these procedures or whatever trauma or gunshots appeared as long as they were not to a persons' head and brain—a specialty not yet developed. The ancillary personnel were gaining experience but also began to feel that things were getting repetitive without new learning. It quickly became clear to everyone that this lack of new learning was a sign that the specially trained people were ready for clinical practice in the real world.

Addie had been successful and hired a male accountant, two single female OR nurses, and one male X Ray technician. It became a point of discussion among the female Kelly group that it would now include three eligible men to be matched with the large incoming class of single eligible female nurses. Brad looked at Addie and said, "now remember you have too many things to do to become the local matchmaker, heh?" Addie answered, "not to worry, it is a 'girl thing' again dear!"

It was a memorable day in late April when the entire Kelly group was summoned to a hospital meeting room. As everyone entered, it was clear that Doctor Huxley, Nurse Kravitz, OR supervisor Fogarty, and a half dozen surgical attendings, especially Doc Davis and Colon, and miscellaneous instructors were sitting behind the podium. As the Kelly group was seated, Addie was heard saying, "wow if this is not an execution, let's hope it is an honorable discharge, heh?"

With the hubbub settling down, Doctor Huxley got up and said, "Thank you for attending. We are gathered here for two reasons. To award you your well-earned certificates and to congratulate each of you on becoming members of the Kelly group."

After a pause, Doc Huxley said, "Brad and Addie, the day you showed up at my office for registration, I knew then that I was in the presence of a powerful and charismatic couple that displayed leadership and commanded respect. Now almost two years later I look at you and this group and I know I was right. Brad and Addie, you have surrounded yourselves with the 'Best of the Best.' Congratulations to all of you." As the entire podium entourage stood up to applause and maintain a standing ovation.

"As I pass out your certificates you will note that they are all framed in the classic diploma black frame with a glass cover ready to be hung up in your hospital lobby where they are available for your patients' perusal. Addie, in case something happens, I entrust to you the duplicate copies for you to store in a water and fireproof safe. As I call each name, I will mention the different certifications that each graduate has earned."

Bradley E Kelly MD.............Doctor of Internal
Medicine and Surgery

Adelle A Kelly RN.................Nursing, OR nurse, and
Assistant Surgery

Tom G Hall MD...................Doctor of Internal
Medicine and Surgery

Sally F Hall RN...................Nursing, OR nurse, and
Assistant Surgery

Daniel B Greene MD...........Pathology, lab
technician, phlebotomy,
anesthesia, IV therapy,
and EKG tech.

Ingrid V Greene RN-NA.....General nursing and
nurse anesthetist

Stanley W Norwood MD.....Doctor of Internal
Medicine and Obstetrics

Cindy O Norwood RN, L&D...Nursing, Labor &
Delivery, and Nursery

Winston O Reinhart MD.....Doctor of Internal
Medicine

Marlene V Reinhart RN-NA....General nursing and
nurse anesthetist

Angus M McKenzie CPA......Certified Medical
Accountant

Susan L Dearwood RN.......Nursing and OR nurse

Lilian N Cross RN...............Nursing and OR nurse

Adriana B Sylvester RN.......Nursing and OR
supervisor

Mary C Beers RN................Nursing and hospital
nursing supervisor

Reginald P Labor RT..........Radiology technician

JD Sinclair............................Certified Purchasing
Agent

"With Mister Sinclair already in the Kelly employ, Doctor Kelly will deliver his certificate. And so that does it. You all have the certification you came here to earn. We will miss you as I said, you are without any doubt the 'Best of the Best' we have graduated in past years. Good luck and remember to always respect and protect your patients. Always stay alert as one day I might suddenly appear in your hospital, heh?"

*

For the next two days, everyone packed. Addie had two projects to get done before she and Brad would have a final gathering at the training center and provide specific instructions for things to do upon arrival at their new hospital. On the fourth day, they all gathered in a private meeting room. Brad started the discussion as he said, "to start with I have a stethoscope for all doctors and nurses. Step up for your own labeled with your name, and pick up your new name tag that matches your certificate and with the Kelly Hospital name. Of note is that Stanley and Cindy have each an extra fetoscope. This year each name tag comes with a lanyard or a magnetic attachment. Your work will decide which system works best for you. Now let's have a chat."

"The hospital and your lodging are ready. Housing wise, move in your luggage and get some limited groceries since you all have three meals a day available at the hospital cafeteria for four bits—that is a free hot or cold lunch, a 15-cent breakfast of unlimited coffee and an egg/cheese sandwich, and a full supper with dessert and unlimited coffee for 35 cents. FYI these charges are our food costs and 10% for labor."

Addie then took over. "Let's talk about standards in our hospital."

OR OFFICES. "The OR nurses and the nursing assistant surgeon share the same office. The OR supervisor has her own office as well as the nurse anesthetist with the anesthesia agents. There is one changing room/water closet for all nurses. There is one doctor's lounge for all surgical and non-surgical doctors. There are two operating rooms and elective surgery is held Mon-Fri from 8AM to 5PM with the last scheduled procedure to start at 2PM. Emergency surgery overrides the elective one!"

THE LOBBY IN THE SQUARE. "There is a welcome and information counter near the main entrance door. It is manned by volunteers from 7AM to 9PM seven days a week. Its purpose is to direct patients and visitors to the appropriate locations and to avoid the least number of people wandering around and end up in the wrong place."

DOCTORS WAITING ROOM. "To avoid a noisy and confusing hub, it is manned by a volunteer from 7AM to 5PM. As any patient arrives, their names are entered into the doctor's list they will be seeing. This is a first come first serve system for now. In the future appointments may take over. Anyways, it is up to the doctor's nurse to come to the waiting room and call the next name on her doctor's list; and cross it out to avoid confusion."

DOCTOR'S HOURS. "FYI, doctors see patients at different times: surgeons see patients from 1-5PM, Doctor Reinhart from 8AM to 5PM minus the noon hour. Doctor Morse sees patients from 1-5PM. Obstetrical patients are seen from 1-5PM—if a delivery interrupts the schedule, every patient is offered to return the next day or wait if there is an immediate need."

WARD NURSES. "Each ward nurse is to stop at the Nursing Supervisor's office each day to get their daily assignments in the three wards—medical, surgical, and post-delivery. Each ward has a changing room and bathroom for nurses. The changing room has key-locked lockers for clothes and valuables. The key belongs on your body and is for the day's use. At the end of the day, leave the key in the locker as you might work in another ward tomorrow. Of note is that eventually each ward will have a shift charge nurse."

"Look around, where are the ward nurses. Well the bulk of graduates were scheduled to graduate in mid-August like we were supposed to as well. We have so far 25 RNs scheduled to join our hospital—17 from Amarillo, and 8 from Dallas. We have been guaranteed that 10 will arrive in one week as early graduates from the top of the class. Another 5 by the 4th of July, and the last 10 by mid-August. That schedule of arrivals should match hospital occupancy."

EMERGENCY WARD NURSES. "We need to name a charge nurse and select the unique nurses from the first crop of arriving nurses. These nurses do not rotate like ward nurses because of their willingness to work in a high anxiety position." Doctor Kelly was now preparing to take over.

DOCTORS HOSPITAL ROUNDS. "Doctors do hospital rounds at different times The medical doctors usually do rounds in the morning. The surgeons and obstetricians do rounds when they are available. The point is that their patients' nurses are expected to be accompanying the doctors to discuss the patient's care and new medical orders."

COMPLAINTS. "All workers who have a complaint or worry; there is a hierarchy to follow. Charge nurse, nurse supervisor, and administrator (that's Addie first and me second, heh)." With plenty of laughter. "The point is that we hope things will get resolved on site before it moves up the chain and makes more waves than necessary. The last category to discuss is fees which we will break down to doctors and hospital fees."

HOSPITAL FEES.

A—Medical Ward. "The daily rate varies from $2-$5 depending on the treatments the patient received. Below are some treatment examples.

Oxygen	Blood transfusions	Drainage
Dressing changes	Oral meds	Chest air trapping
IV fluids	IM meds	Blood testing labs
Foley catheter	Colostomy care	Naso-gastric tube
Chest PT	EKG testing	X Rays

"As you can imagine there is a fee for each treatment plus the number of days each was given. Of note the highest fee is for X Rays as an upright chest or abdomen or any fracture view is 50 cents apiece!"

B—Operating Room. "The standard usage fee for a 1-2-hour procedure is $6 and it's an all-inclusive fee that includes OR nurse, nurse anesthetist and anesthesia, IV fluids, one blood transfusion if necessary, Oxygen, incisional dressing, and all surgical instruments, garments, and miscellaneous items. We hope that a three-day stay for an operation will cost the patient $10 plus the surgeon's fees."

C—Labor and delivery. "This is another inclusive fee--$3 for both labor and delivery. Post-delivery ward care is also an inclusive $2 a day fee, as the nursery fee is 25 cents a day. This is another example that a three day stay in the hospital to have a baby is +-$10. The Obstetrician fee is separate."

DOCTORS FEES.

"It is not new, doctors do not work for free. Time is money and the years of training command a fair compensation for services."

A—The Office call. "The charge is $2/15-30 minutes, $3/45 minutes, and $4/60 minutes."

B—Treatment room. "Depending on the extent of each procedure it varies from $2 to $4 to $6."

C—Fracture room. "A simple fracture with setting and casting is $5."

D—Med/surg ward care. "Doctor's daily ward rounds are $2. There are no doctor charges for post-op-care as that is included in the surgeon's fee as well as one post discharge office visit. Any extra ward visits are also $2 per visit."

E—Surgical fees. "Surgical fees fall in four categories based on degree of complexity and time."

Routine.........Appendectomy.............$25
High risk........C-Section.................$40
Complex.........Cholecystectomy..........$50
Complex and long.......Bowel resection with colostomy.........$75

F—Obstetrical fees. "This is an inclusive fee that includes pre delivery visits, labor and delivery, post-delivery care, and newborn care—all for $35 unless there is a C-Section. A miscarriage D&C charge is $15."

Addie took over, "that does it for now. We will see you at the Kelly Memorial Hospital. We will have another meeting after we know you are all present, have toured and examined every corner of your new digs, and are ready to go to work, heh!"

*

The Duo took the red eye and arrived at their new home by 10AM. After unpacking their coffee, snacks, clothing and personals, the Duo headed for the hospital for a quick tour with Mike and JD before the noon cafeteria opened up. "Well hello, so glad to see you. Let me guide you around. Shall we start with the doctors' wing?" "Sure, what is this?" JD stepped up and said, "I presumed that everyone had forgotten that a hospital has a pharmacy and pharmacist to dispense meds to inpatients as well as retailing to outpatients. It was Doctor Morse's idea to use the unassigned empty room next to the Administrator's Office and add a retailing counter with the medication shelves behind the pharmacist's worktable."

Addie added, "so where do we find a pharmacist this late in the game?" "Look behind you!" "Hello Ma'am, you must be Missus Kelly and you must be Doctor Kelly, my name is Frank Libby, registered pharmacist in Texas and recent college roommate to JD. "JD then admitted that a recent graduate of Frank's caliber could do both jobs. So I hired him, paid him my salary, and put him up in the unoccupied apartment next to mine. Frank knows this is a temporary appointment and requires your approval to become a permanent job." Brad then added, "well let's have a chat. After a coffee in the Administrator's office, it became clear that this guy's personality would fit with all the female workers plus, coming from El Paso, he was also fluent in Spanish. Offered the other benefits, free housing for one year, and a guaranteed salary of $67.31 every two weeks; the deal was sealed with a handshake.

Moving along the Duo walked into Brad's office and treatment room. Addie said, "that is beautiful furniture to include a desk, two patient chairs, three metal filing cabinets, several wood bookshelves, and one classic examination chair/table. The treatment room had a steel alloy table, metal shelves and closed cabinets. A quick review of the other doctor's offices revealed they were similarly furnished. There was a telephone room every other doctor's office as well as a doctor and nurse's place to work the medical records. Opposite the doctors' offices was the accountant's room which had been furnished with a desk, filing cabinets, ledgers, and a current model Remington typewriter with reams of papers. The Administrator and purchasing agent's room had already been seen.

As they were leaving the doctor's wing, Doc Morse showed up with a wagon full of unopened boxes of modern meds. "I have decided that I no longer plan to dispense meds, like not do deliveries, and no more appendectomies. I want to only do medicine and if some cases are too complicated I will refer them to Doc Reinhart, heh? But other than that, I can't wait to move in after you announce its grand opening." Brad looked at Addie and said, "grand opening, we didn't plan for that!" "True, but it can easily be arranged, heh?"

The next area was the operating room and surgical ward. As the Duo approached, Brad stopped short of entering. "Mike we forgot something. We need a surgical waiting area where family and close friends can wait to hear how the surgery went for their loved ones." "Yes, the boys will add one this afternoon— right close to the wing's entry."

Brad was all smiles as he walked thru the operating rooms, nurses' quarters, the sterilizing room, and the recovery room. He looked at Mike and only said, "well done!" Walking into the ward he noticed the high ceilings and large windows in each double patient rooms—to control summer heat. Each room had a water closet and sink, electrical outlets, oxygen ports, and overhead lighting with a bedside table and nightlight. The big eye catcher was the walls and ceilings with hardwood panels. Mike said, "we could not use tongue and groove as we did in the square. We needed something that could wash off body fluids. So, since plaster/slats were impractical, we went with prefab panels that we varnished and sanded so to make the walls washable." As they walked down the center aisle, Addie noted a red light over the patient doors. She asked what it was for as Mike said, "see the red switch over the bedside table. Well a flick of the switch and the light comes on to call a nurse." At the end of the surgical ward was the locked pharmacy, a nurses' station with a changing room, general storage, a charge nurse's office, a handheld telephone, and miscellaneous cabinets and counters. That is when

Addie said, "JD, would you order a percolator/electric stove at each ward's nurses' station."

The next ward to visit was the medical ward which was a duplicate of the surgical ward except for the 5-bed patient ward plus a larger bathing room— which matched the square footage of the operating theatre in the surgical ward. This time, Addie had another epiphany. Looking at the nurses' station, she realized that eventually a unit secretary would be needed to answer the phone, do prep paperwork, and other nursing jobs.

The next ward was the combination labor and delivery, post-birth rooms, and the nursery. It was well designed for both the nurses, the gals in labor, and nursing moms. Stepping out, the tour headed for the cafeteria wing. First the tour walked down the hall to see how central supply was filling up. JD was a meticulous person as all the supplies were well labelled. Brad asked, "is this all replacements?" "Yes, the wards are packed to the top and these two rooms are the daily replacements. This is where I do my inventories to do timely ordering. Being the only medical facility within hundreds of miles, we must never run out of essential supplies or I will be sent walking down the road to out of town, heh?"

Next was lunch. The Duo introduced themselves to Mike's aunt and admired the all-steel alloyed kitchen. Choosing a cold roast beef sandwich and coffee, the Duo admired the upgraded tables for two, four, and eight people. The dining room had a relaxing atmosphere. Once adjusted, the Duo continued a discussion with Mike, JD, and Frank.

"So we missed the dental room, and still have to check out the X Ray department, the Emergency Ward, the laboratory, and where did the fracture room go to?" "Well let's talk about the fracture room. It was planned to be next to the dental room but Doc Morse thought that was a bad idea with all the dust it creates next to the open square. Then he pointed out that most fractures appear in the Emergency Department, so why not put the fracture room right there in that department." Brad admitted it was a good idea and would check it out later.

Going back on their steps they walked into the dental room, The chair went up and down as the upper body went back. There was some chloroform in a cabinet and several packs of different extraction forceps. Most important, the room was soundproof. The X Ray department had a fixed X Ray tube and upright frames to hold an X Ray plate. Extremities were placed on the table for front to side views to locate the fracture depth.

It was clear that this machine was fixed to this room and not a portable one to go all over the hospital. Plus the walls were lined with lead sheathing to prevent radiation escaping to workers, patients, or visitors,

Next was the Emergency Ward. It had its own entrance from the square or from the outside ambulance driveway. It was roomy with four rolling stretchers separated by sliding curtains. The fracture room was well stocked with a real fracture table to allow proper alignment of the proximal and distal bones. There were the usual nurses' station, nurses' changing room, a pharmacy, a storage room, and oxygen ports everywhere.

Heading to their last department, to their surprise, Doctor Greene was there to greet them. Addie said, "well hello, we didn't think anyone would be here today. How did you manage to be here?" "Jumped on a coal freight train at 3AM with Ingrid and spent the night in the caboose with the bold brakemen." Brad was surprised and took advantage of the situation. "Well, in that case, tell us what tests you have the equipment or knowledge to perform." "Be glad to, the list I've prepared includes ABO blood typing and transfusion compatibility tests, blood sugar, electrolytes, Bun/Creatine, liver SGPT and fractionated bilirubin, pancreatic amylase, inflammatory sed rate, CBC and peripheral smear exam, Urinalysis and smear exam, gross organ ID, tissue histology, sputum smear analysis for bacteria type, TB, or virus type pattern. Last of all I will add the EKG testing as soon as we get a machine. Plus you know that I will do the phlebotomy, start IV's, and perform all blood transfusions. And as a last resort, I will do the rare anesthesia case, especially the one procedure anesthetists hate—the combating patient in the dental room, heh?"

With the tour finished, Brad verified that the final account was paid off and that the hospital, Doctor's Row, and apartment house were paid off and ready to open; as soon as the help got here, had their own tours, and got accustomed to their domain.

*

That night the Duo had their first business meeting in their huge bathtub. Addie started. "We have been lucky to fill most essential positions. But we are missing several ward and Emergency Ward shift charge nurses. These positions should be filled with experienced nurses, don't you think?" "Absolutely and we have several RNs who are transferring from Dallas, and we should be able to work with Mary Beers, the nursing supervisor/director, to find the most experienced nurses." "Ok, let's hope that solves the problem." "So what else do you want to discuss?" "Money!" "Oh no, my most disliked subject. Do we have to?"

"Yes, it is a matter of our personal bank account and what to do with people who cannot pay our medical fees." "Ok, well let's talk about reality. I started with my $100,000 inheritance, we added your $15,000 from the sale of your ranch. We then spent $50,000 for the land and the hospital, $12,000 for Doctors Row and $6,000 for the apartment. My calculations show a bank balance of say +- $45,000!" "I agree." Brad continued, "I suggest we put $10,000 in the hospital account to backup operations till we generate income, $30,000 left in our personal account, and $5,000 in a special account to pay hospital and doctor fees that people cannot honestly afford. That way our services are always paid for."

"Well that is certainly noble, but who will decide who the lucky recipients will be?" "We chose Angus McKenzie as the accountant. Not only because he could handle the numbers, but because he had a gentle way about him. I trust his judgement and if he pays off someone's bill out of the account, I will never contest it." "So we are giving him the right to withdraw money out of this fund?" "Yes, and he has one year to deplete the account before we decide what to do next year depending on the hospital and doctor incomes." "I like it. I knew you would know what to do, just like knowing all my trigger points, heh?" "Well let me at a few of them for priming the pump, heh?"

The next morning during their replenishing breakfast, Addie asked what their agenda for the day looked like. "In the next two days, most of our workers will arrive. JD and Frank will be touring people all day and we'll be around to answer anyone's questions after their tour and inspection of their own domain. Plus, we hope to choose those charge nurses assuming Mary Beers arrives with the personal files of those nurse transfers and graduates."

By 10AM, JD and Frank were hot on the tour trail. The Duo was watching workers arrive, walk about on the tour, and clearly express their individual "shock and awe" as the smiles were abundant. The Duo watched Angus view his own office, the OR nurses see the operating theater, and see the many young nurses totally amazed at the hospital structure. After the tour the Duo met with Angus. "In my life I never imagined getting my own office in the wide-open spaces, why I expected to be put in the cellar like most accountants expect to be." After realizing that JD had fully furnished the office, Brad added, "If there are other things you need, have JD get them for you. Now let us tell you about a special fund ... that you will be able to draw from... More on this later."

Retrospectively, the most dramatic workers that were near collapsing were Tom and Sally Hall, Winston and Marlene Reinhart, and Stanley and Cindy Norwood—the three doctors in private practice. It was clear that their entire training and career had depended on trusting Addie and Brad to make their new home and practice location in a modern hospital setting with a new house to boot. It was that night that the three Doctors and their wives made clear their total acceptance of their presumed long-term digs.

The last worker to arrive that first day was Mary Beers. Sitting down in the administrator's office, Mary presented several nurses that would be capable

The New Western Doctor | 195

of being a shift charge nurse because of training excellence and years of experience. After a lengthy meeting, the nine ward shift charge nurses were chosen because of at least two years of experience. The one exception was a young nurse out of the high school graduating class. The one called, Nancy Grover RN, had recommendations from at least six instructors or nurse supervisors, and the highest recommendation was from Nurse Kravitz. She was hired without interviewing her as the Emergency Ward's daytime charge nurse.

That night, the Duo was having a second hot tub meeting. "It looks like tomorrow, Thursday, will bring the leftover workers. So what do you think about placing an ad in the Friday paper that we are having an open house on Saturday and Sunday?" "That sounds great, that means that Friday we will have a 10AM meeting with all our workers and answer a ton of questions as we inform them that all department heads will need to be present in their domain to answer the public's questions during the open house." "Sounds like a plan." After some pausing, Brad asked, "so are you open for business tonight?" "Sure but as usual, what you bring in you take out, heh?"

Thursday was as expected, every worker showed up plus a total of eight Dallas transfer nurses and seven RN graduates. Mary made quick work of assigning each nurse. As directed by Addie, the first day of operations would be Monday morning and all workers were asked to be in their domain to get things organized.

Now it was Friday morning and the Duo was having their usual replenishing breakfast in the cafeteria, while getting ready for the 10AM meeting.

*

With everyone seated in the dining room, the first question came from Sally.

Sally—"If there is a bad case and the two surgeons decide to tackle it by working together, then what happens to you and me?"

Addie—"Well I will turn to administrative duties, but you will be reassigned by Mary to help somewhere

where extra help is needed. Since you are qualified as an RN first, you can do the work anywhere in this hospital. I will admit that your daily renumeration will reflect your current pay scale."

Ingrid—"On the same note, with one case on, what happens to the extra OR nurse?"

Addie—"same as Sally. You will be reassigned. The key to remember is that no RN will be left floundering or sent home. If push comes to shove and your nursing skills are not needed, then we will find some work for you while helping the purchasing agent, accountant, or the pharmacist."

Doctor Norwood—"it is easy to see teams like Kelly/Hall and Reinhart/Morse but what happens to Doctor Greene and me. Who will share night call with us?"

Brad—"no one, unless you want an Obstetrician to start doing lab tests or Doctor Greene to start delivering babies." General laughter. "The bottom line, in time both doctors will have a partner when the hospital business picks up. Until then, it is what it is and all of us will try to minimize your workload after 5PM!"

Doctor Reinhart—"when Marlene is busy providing anesthesia, what am I to do without an office nurse since I have office hours all day?"

Brad—"we have already worked that out with Mary. We will choose three RN that are willing to do office work instead of ward nursing. Mary will train them and the three will rotate in your employ free of charge.

Nurse Grover—"you have told me that the EW (emergency ward) will be manned 24 hours a day. So who will work the evening shift (5PM to Midnight), and the night shift (Midnight to 7AM)?"

Addie—"Mary is currently reviewing files on the eight transferring nurses from Dallas. It looks like several have worked those two shifts with EW experience. We hope to fill those two spots before Monday."

Unnamed RN—"if we are sick or have personal issues, and we cannot come to work; what do we do?"

Addie—"Between 6AM to 7AM, call the hospital and have the volunteer desk transfer your call to Mary's office. If you don't have a phone, send someone with the same message, or use a street corner phone."

Unnamed RN—"if we come to work but there are not enough patients to care for, what happens to us?" "If Mary cannot find you a nursing spot for the day, she will send you home. As long as you showed up for assignment, you will receive full pay while at home. Remember one thing, you are an RN, not a housekeeper."

Unnamed charge nurse—"how do we order supplies that are running low?"

Addie—"there is a box labeled 'purchasing' at each nursing station. JD will visit each box twice a day at 11AM and 3PM. If you need something 'right now,' then call him on the telephone."

Unnamed RN—"what do we do if a patient confides in us that he or she cannot pay for their medical care?"

Brad—"notify Angus and request that he do a private visit with the patient. If this is a legitimate situation, Angus has avenues he can take."

Reginald Labor—"not to bring up the issue again, but since I am the only X Ray tech, am I to be on call each night?"

Brad—"absolutely not, every medical worker needs to have at least every other night free of call!" There was a very silent pause as everyone was waiting for a solution. "I have known a long time ago, a person in this room that is certified as an X Ray technician. That is Doctor Greene who is already overworked and without anyone to take his call. For now, he will alternate with you as the X Ray tech. I assure you, you will have a coworker as soon as the hospital business picks up."

With no further questions, Addie said, "we have two very important informative issues to present. So let's take a 10-minute break and we'll return for those two very important issues, heh."

CHAPTER 8

The Early Hospital Practice

"I assume you have visited the bathroom and all got a fresh cup of coffee. From past experiences, usually during an intermission, people talk and new questions come up. So before I present my two issues, does anyone have any questions?" "Yes!"

Anonymous RN—"could we have a cork bulletin board in this dining room?"

Addie—"Yes, of course. JD would you obtain one, and add four headings such as wanted, for sale, hospital news, and miscellaneous. Plus clean it up every two weeks since these boards tend to fill up with ads that have expired or are old news."

Nancy Grover RN—'is there anyone in this hospital, other than Doctor Greene, who can start an IV?"

Brad—"Yes. In an emergency all docs can start an IV. It will get an emergency case to the OR till a transfusion is ready."

Anonymous RN—"what are we to do if a medication runs out in the ward pharmacy?"

Addie—"call your night supervisor. She will have the general pharmacy key and will get what you need." "But wait, 'what night super,' we don't have any do we?"

Brad—"you are correct. We are now advertising in many Texas 75-bed hospitals for experienced nurses to fill the vacancy. These unique nurses must be able to help anyone in any ward—especially the labor and delivery unit since it is difficult for one RN to manage two gals in very active labor. Until we hire a total of three to fill the 24/7 5PM-Midnight evening shift and the Midnight-7AM night shift, we suggest that you use your shift charge nurse who will have the key to the general pharmacy."

After a long pause, Addie took over. "Recently Mary made an important observation. In her words, 'you have candlestick phones everywhere in this hospital, but very few people know how to use them!' So listen well. To call outside the hospital in town, you take the ear receiver off the hook, click the hook twice, and the outside operator will come on. Give her the exchange and number, as the hospital is MED-1, and the operator will connect you. If you don't remember the exchange or number, use the phonebook which is situated under the phone."

Brad then took over. "We have 20 phones situated in this building and with 20 numbers. Look at the card we passed out. If you want the pharmacy, place your finger in #5 and swing the dial to its end. The phone will then ring in the pharmacy. Now look at your card. There are the 20 locations and its dialing number. Take a look at it."

1 Doc Kelly house, 2 Doc Hall house, 3 Doc Morse house, 4 Doc Reinhart house, 5 Doc Greene house, 6 Doc Norwood house, 7 Front welcome desk, 8 Medical ward, 9 Surgical ward, 0 OR, 1-2 EW, 1-3 Maternity ward, 1-4 Purchasing 1-5 Pharmacy, 1-6 Accounting, 1-7 Nursing office/night super, 1-8 Doctor's wing, 1-9 Administrator, 1-0 Labor and Delivery.

Addie took over. "If no one answers, use your feet and walk over or send a messenger. As a last resort, call the front desk and have them send a volunteer to find the person you are looking for. And as human nature would have it, if you can't remember the number, or don't have your card with you, then lift the phone, tip it over, and look at the base. That is right, a hospital phone card is glued to the base of each phone in this building!"

After a long pause and dozens of comments. Brad shocked everyone by saying, "does anyone realize what it would be like in this hospital if there was a train derailment and a couple dozen injured patients would be brought in by wagons. DO YOU KNOW

WHERE YOU SHOULD BE PLACED TO GET
THE MOST OUT OF YOUR TRAINING. Well such
an event is called a disaster and the hospital will
go into a Code D Status. The welcome desk will
call all doctors, nurses, and ancillary staff that are
not working. When you arrive, go directly to your
designated station, and stay there till the triage officer
sends you elsewhere. Look at the sheet that Addie
is passing out. This is the master list and it will be
posted on our new bulletin board."

Nancy Grover RN	Receiving triage officer.
Doc Kelly	OR scrubbed and gowned. Ready to operate.
Doc Hall	Same as Doc Kelly.
Doc Norwood	EW to start IVs.
Doc Morse	Fracture room.
Doc Greene	EW to start IVs and draw blood for typing.
Doc Reinhart	EW for control of blood loss and medical Rx.

OR nurses	OR ready to prep surgical tools.
OR super	Pre-op.
Night super	EW providing general nursing assignments.
Anesthetist RN	OR ready to provide anesthesia.
Medical ward RN	Medical ward caring for head injuries.
Surgical ward RN	EW, to be assigned by night super.
Purchasing agent	Stretcher orderly.
Accountant	Stretcher orderly.
Pharmacy	Medication and IV bottle distribution.
Surgical charge nurses	Post-op care in recovery room.
X Ray	Remain in department ready to take films.
Assistant surgeons	Gowned and ready to operate.

Nursing supervisor	Caring for post op surgical ward patients with skeleton crew.
Labor and delivery RN	Standby in EW in case of injured pregnant gals. If none, will be reassigned to help surgical nurses in EW.

There was total silence in the room. Addie shocked everyone as she took a school bell and wrung it loud and clear. After most workers nearly fell off their chairs, she said, "if there is a Code D called, it will not be a practice. Believe this bell sound and if you are home, the volunteer will only verify your name and then say Code D, repeat Code D, and then hang up. Don't bother calling back to verify, just get over here!"

Brad then addressed the group as he said, "tomorrow we are having an open house and everyone is expected to be in their domain greeting people and answering questions. See you in the morning for a free breakfast."

*

Gathering in the cafeteria for breakfast, Mary Beers suggested that instead of letting visitors wander all over the hospital, that Addie be the greeter and for each 12-15 visitors, that she assigns a standby department head to guide the group and answer all their questions. Shortly thereafter the visitors started arriving. At first it was old home day. Everyone knew Addie and had to hug her and carry on a nostalgic reunion. Eventually Brad took one group as Tom took the second group. Then the groups were less reminiscent of Addie as a rancher and things were more orderly.

Brad had already toured two groups when he lined up to take the next group. Addie was very vocal when she said, "well if it isn't Mayor Ulyssis Monroe, his town council, Sheriff Sam Butler, Judge Gagnon, and the bank's President Homer Rankin. You are all in luck as your tour guide is Doctor Kelly."

Brad started the tour like he had done the other two, but soon the questions got oriented towards money. Mayor Monroe got on the band wagon early when he said, "this is clearly an expensive undertaking. You have not asked us for a city contribution, a tax abatement, a bank loan, or a county's contribution of Federal funds. Why?" "As I said at our wedding reception, this is my parents' gift to you. Now, depending on our bottom line after 12 months of operation, well that may become another matter. So we will see. I am sure you are all aware that towns often need to subsidize hospitals that often have to provide free care to the less fortunate town residents." "Yes we agree, and if you see the need before 12 months, kindly let us know. For now, your property taxes have been cancelled for the next two years just so you know we want you here and are willing to financially help if needed."

Judge Gagnon then added, "and I will be sure to congratulate my son-in-law for his great architectural designs. This is a beautiful building, well laid out, the center of medical and surgical care, a real Emergency

Ward, and with all the doctors' offices in one wing right next to a commercial pharmacy—excellent, simply excellent."

Hordes of people kept arriving all day. By 5PM, the doors were closed and every worker was invited to a full free supper in the cafeteria. After a restful night, everyone was back at 6AM to enjoy their free breakfast of ham, eggs, home fries, toast, and coffee.

The morning was slow as most churches were having services, but at 1PM, ranchers and homesteaders, who had traveled to town for church services, flooded the hospital main entrance. No one was going back home without seeing this talked about modern hospital and meet some of the doctors and nurses.

It was Addie who later summarized things. "Well folks, the open house is done, we have trained to provide medical care for this town, and that is what we will do come morning, heh?" A voice from the back said, "here—here!"

*

When 8AM came, Doctor Reinhart already had a patient waiting. It was a 50-year-old woman with multiple organ failure from some unknown disease. Doctor Reinhart explained it as some strange process that was attacking her organs. It was clear that the only treatment was to treat as many of the symptoms that were debilitating but that there was no known cure for the disease. Throughout the day, Doc Morse sent one of these enigmas each hour for the next two days. During this time he admitted five for treatments that were mostly on the edge of experimental but had shown some benefits in controlling symptoms.

Doctors Kelly and Hall were both seeing patients that had chronic symptoms that could have been ended if the patients had had surgery. Being 250 miles to Albuquerque and 350 miles to Dallas had been the excuse for patients to live with their conditions as was the norm in the 1800s when the local country doctor only did emergency appendectomies—and not always under sterile technique.

Doc Kelly's first patient had an inguinal hernia which allowed loops of intestine to fall thru under minimal strain. He had worn a homemade belt with a pad over the hernia so he could continue working in the fields. Doc Kelly asked a revealing question, "so what made you decide to get this fixed?" "Because I can no longer have relations without a hunk of bowel getting in the way!" "Good enough reason for me. We will get your blood type, check some blood tests, and you will be the first case tomorrow morning. Tonight take a bath and only have 'jello' and liquids after 5PM and only limited water after midnight. If I was you I would shave your pubic hair around your hernia or the OR supervisor nurse will do it for you before surgery." "EEECK, I don't relish the idea of anyone sweeping a razor around my member, heh? I will do it myself and thanks for the warning."

Doctor Kelly's second patient was a 45-year-old woman who had had gall bladder attacks since the birth of her last child. The attacks had become more severe, last longer, and associated with fever. Doc Morse had pushed for surgery, but this patient was not about to leave her six kids. So, blood tests were ordered as Doctor Kelly agreed to see her again this afternoon after her test results were available.

The blood tests showed a high white cell count, slightly elevated pancreatic amylase, and a fractionated bilirubin high in direct bilirubin. When he met with the patient he said, "your clinical exam with tenderness over your gall bladder and your blood tests show a chronic infection with pancreatic irritation. It is also clear that you not only have stones in your gall bladder but also likely have a stone stuck in your bile duct to your intestine. This calls for immediate surgery and we will perform it tomorrow by 10AM. This is what you need to do to get ready … "

Brad was done seeing office patients by 1PM. He was preparing his History and Physical form for the operative charts as Addie was doing administrative work; when a desperate looking EW head nurse showed up and said, "we have just admitted a gut-shot victim who is requesting laudanum for pain control so he can die in peace." "Well Nancy, that was the old way, but it doesn't have to be that way anymore. Get Addie and let's go see the patient."

When the patient saw Addie he said, "Lordy be, it has been years since you were in grade school and I would play poker with your dad." After Dumas Gregory explained his request, Addie said, "you don't have to die Mister Gregory, my husband is a surgeon and he can repair the holes in your intestines and remove the bullet. Here he is, let him explain what he can do."

After a long chat, Brad made the decisive statement. "So with at least an 80% chance, we can save you. You will be asleep thru the procedure and when you wake up in recovery, I will be there to tell you what we did, and the chance of your survival—and without any bull-ticky to minimize the facts." After a real staring match, Dumas Gregory said, "well if you put it that way, I don't have a choice do I Addie?" "Well without surgery you will die for certainty, so why not let us try to save you—that is what we are trained for. Bottom line is this, dying from gut-shots is a lot more painful than recovering from surgery." "Got it, let's go for it."

The surgery proceeded as soon as Doc Greene started an IV and gave him a quick liter of saline, took some basic blood tests, and did the usual ABO blood typing. An Xray located the bullet in the patient's left paraspinal muscles. Under chloroform anesthesia with a premedication of IM scopolamine, the procedure started. With a long incision from two inches below the sternum to three inches below the navel, the surgeons entered the abdomen. There were no bullet holes visible but the surgeons knew that running the small intestine would reveal several. The colon was free of bullet holes so a colostomy bag would not be needed.

Brad went for the bullet and easily removed it from the paraspinal muscles. Then they started 'running' the bowel from the duodenum as first part of the small intestine to the last part called the ileum before the small intestine joined with the large colon. Brad found the first two holes and quickly over sutured the two holes with 1-0 cotton sutures. Brad found the second hole but missed the next one as Addie, who was doing her own 'run' found it. Brad said, "good for you and the patient." The team found two more holes to repair. Once done, Brad removed the appendix since a stone could be felt in it and would eventually cause a case of acute appendicitis.

Waiting in the recovery room, Brad's first words when the patient was clearly awake were, "too bad for you, you will have to continue living." Over the next week, Dumas Gregory had incisional pain as expected and with the morphine he could not take care of himself. In the first 24 hours he needed the 'red snake' catheter for urinary retention, could not wipe himself after nature's call, and needed help to walk to the bathroom and get out of bed. The second day things were better and he was allowed to have sips of water. The third day, things were looking up. The patient was independent and was allowed 'jello' feedings every two hours and as much water as tolerated. It was the fifth day when soft puddings and oatmeal were allowed. The incision was healing well and he was offered discharge on the seventh day. The patient refused to leave.

Mister Gregory's point was, "I have been well cared for and given a new lease on life. I want to stay here till I am back to normal. I will pay the daily hospital rate of $6 and pay for all the nurses salaries working this ward till I am good and ready to leave." Brad's decision was clear, "hey if he wants to waste his savings, then we'll take his money especially when we are still working on building a decent hospital census, heh?"

Addie started laughing. "Well Brad, there is an advantage to being raised in this town. Dumas Gregory is likely the richest man in town as he has a productive gold mine." Brad looked at Addie and said, "well there are two ways to look at that. Not knowing these social issues, one has a more neutral opinion of patients' personalities and can treat the illness as its own entity. I am glad you did not tell me of Gregory's wealth before we started the procedure. Let's maintain that approach in the future; just like the other doctors have the same luxury, heh?"

*

Looking back at the other doctors, it was Doc Norwood who could not believe his fortune. Doc Morse had sent his fifteen pregnant gals to see him. One by one, he did a complete medical and obstetrical evaluation and accepted all fifteen future moms. Most were due within four months and two were due within a week.

It was a transitional time for birthing. Gals wanted pain relief during hard labor and during the birth. Morphine could not be used because of the risk of respiratory depression in the newborn. So many ladies were given an injection of scopolamine which provided some sedation and amnesia, but often caused ladies in labor to go 'BANANAS' and rant and rave like banshees. So an alternative was natural labor with a terminal breathing of ether which was less toxic than chloroform to mother and baby. If inhaled at the proper time, would not enter the newborn's circulation as the cord was clamped as early as possible."

Doc Hall was the unknown surgeon in town. Although his cases lagged a bit, his true nature was quickly realized, when a rare situation arose. Brad was busy doing an emergency bowel obstruction, during afternoon office hours, when his patients were left waiting. Without hesitating, Tom started seeing Brad's patients. The classic office call went this way.

"Hello Mister and Missus Taylor, I am the other surgeon in town. Doctor Kelly is in the OR doing an emergency case. If it is Ok with you, I will obtain your history, do an exam, order some pre-op labs if necessary, and schedule you for surgery. Doctor Kelly and Addie will be seeing you the morning of surgery while you are in pre-op and I assure you that they will do your operation."

The gentleman gave his wife the nod. Missus Taylor then said, 'we have known Addie since she was in school but maybe it will be easier to discuss the reason for surgery. So let's proceed." "Very well, what is the problem?" "I am 45 years old, have six healthy kids, we cannot afford any more, I have very heavy menstrual bleeding that puts me to be bed for a week and I assure you those are not easy days for a hard- working husband. Plus Doc Morse has told me for years that I have a uterine fibroid." The husband finally said, "it is time that something is done for we can no longer have relations without causing my wife a lot of pain." After doing a complete exam, Doc Hall wrote the operative diagnosis as 'uterine fibroid, menstrual hemorrhaging, anemia, and dyspareunia. The operation was a partial hysterectomy. As he said, "your surgery will be done in three days, these are the blood tests you should do today, and my wife will tell you what you need to do to prepare for your hysterectomy. It has been a pleasure to meet you and good luck with your surgery."

As the Taylors were leaving the Missus asked, "why a partial instead of a complete hysterectomy?" Tom took the time to explain that it was the custom of the times to not enter the birth canal to remove the cervix which was the uterus portion in the birth canal. The reason being the less chance for a post-operative infection. As the husband added, "and I don't mind saying that I need that stimulation to spill my seed, heh?" The next morning Mister Taylor called the OR and changed the surgeon of record to Doctor Hall.

Over weeks, Doc Morse was quickly reestablishing a niche for himself. He had a natural talent for manipulating and reducing closed fractures to oppose fracture sites. Plus he could mold plaster to a smooth finish. In addition, it happened naturally when he admitted two patients: one with lobar pneumonia and the other with viral pneumonia. He admitted both for chest physiotherapy for drainage, used SSKI to loosen secretions, ordered epinephrine injections for excessive mucous production and freely used oxygen. When he discussed both cases with Winston, he wondered if the cases would best be treated by Winston. Winston reviewed both and freely admitted that he had no other treatments to offer and with his heavy census of sick medical patients with many cases of congestive heart failure (CHF), that Doc Morse should continue the course.

Doctor Reinhart could not believe the many cases of CHF. It was clear that 75% of those cases had a history of a heart attack during the past two years. The patients were admitted to give their hearts a rest. The treatment at the time was to start digitalis oral therapy, provide continuous oxygen, intermittent epi injections, a short course of injected mercurial diuretics, and teaching each patient to follow a low sodium diet as well as maintaining a low body weight. Generally, a week in the hospital stabilized these patients. As an outpatient, the patients were maintained on oral digitalis and their diet. Periodically when peripheral edema and chest fluid worsened, the patients would come to the office to receive a mercurial diuretic injection as toxic as it was in itself.

On the surgical side, both surgeons were busy with trauma and elective surgery. Both were maintaining a surgical ward with a stable census of 15 patients. The census was maintained by keeping some temporary colostomy patients in the hospital till the colostomy was closed. For patients who had a permanent colostomy, they were discharged once they demonstrated an ease in the bag's care.

Doctor Greene was kept as busy any doctor could handle. On top of it all, he was advertising in the local paper a $5 payment for anyone who would register their ABO blood type and be willing to be on an 'on call' list for blood type specific transfusions. If they were called and their blood was taken for a transfusion, they would receive another $5 for a unit of blood. That was how Doc Greene was able to quickly find blood type specific blood before blood refrigeration was possible. On top of all his duties, he was the official doctor to handwrite an Xray report to put in the patient's outpatient or inpatient chart.

Doc Norwood was popular with pregnant patients and was drawing a clientele from neighboring communities. As is often the case, he performed an emergency C-Section on a bleeding gal while in labor. Saving a mother and a healthy baby, when faced with a deadly 'placenta previa' hemorrhage, spread like wildfire. In a similar situation, faced with a mom bleeding to death from a hypotonic uterus after the birth, it was Doc Kelly and Addie who performed an emergency hysterectomy under chloroform anesthesia right there in the delivery room. Because of those two cases, people all over the county were coming in for a hospital delivery—paying the price for security and a living mom and healthy baby.

At the end of a month, the hospital medical and surgical wards were 75% full, the maternity ward was a constant flow of new moms and babies, the EW was in constant use with trauma and acute illnesses, and the OR was in full use each mornings. The bottom line was that the hospital was showing figures in the black.

*

That evening the Duo had a meeting in their six-foot-long tub. Addie started, "well we were lucky to find charge nurses in all wards and all three shifts from the working RNs. Mary worked hard and ended up with 'keepers.' Now we finally have three ladies who will be arriving from all over Texas to apply for the 'night super' position. These are very important for any hospital's survival, so I want you to be with me when we interview them." "Yep, I agree, I will be there. What else?" "Larger hospitals have a gift shop where they serve coffee and pastries, have gifts that visitors like to give their friends or loved ones, and have a choice of popular novels to sell." "Right now, the library comes in and hands out books to our inpatients, so what is the advantage?" "It is two bits to buy a popular western novel like the 'Dynamo Kid' series by Chet Wilder (The Plains Storyteller) and it makes a perfect affordable gift for their family and friends." "Ok, I like the idea. We'll talk to Mike and find a spot in the square to erect a gift shop. Anything else?" "No! except for … !" "That will have to wait, now it's my turn."

Brad paused, "I have been watching the RNs and when we get to 100% occupancy, there is no way they can care for our patients without having someone answer that damn phone. It is time to add a 'unit clerk' to answer the phone, take care of preparing charts, adding new lab results, preparing purchasing orders, and I am certain several other duties can be found for them." "Agree, agree, and agree. Plus I know where we can find them!" "Where and how many do we need?" "High school students and we need three for days and three for evenings." "Well, if you agree to find them and train them, I will now attend to your needs, heh?" "As I recall, my needs are your same needs; are they not?" "Probably!"

The next morning they hired Mike to build a gift shop and arranged for a salesman to provide gifts and books. Addie arranged for a meeting with high school juniors and seniors to offer them a job as unit clerk, and Brad had a short surgical case. The Duo was ready for the 10AM interviews. The first one was with a 50-year-old widow who wanted to work four evenings or nights a week and wanted the weekends off. Addie started the interview. "Welcome, I read your request and so tell us about you,"

"My name is Agatha Woodrow and I go by the name of Aggie. I am moving to Amarillo because my daughter and her husband live here and I want to spend time with my two beautiful granddaughters ages 3 and 5. I can work with any nurse and I am able to work anywhere is a hospital including the labor and delivery or EW department." The Duo asked, how many babies have you delivered?" "More than I can remember!" After a congenial visit, the lady was hired.

The second applicant was a 49-year-old spinstress by the name of Evelina Bradburry. She wanted to build a retirement fund and get out of a rough Dallas neighborhood. She was eager to work extra shifts if possible; only to build her retirement fund. Qualifying on all parameters, she was hired for the night shift which had a bonus of $10 a week for working either six or seven shifts a week.

The third applicant was a childless 45-year-old married lady by the name of Rose Winslet whose husband was being transferred to Dallas as a Railroad executive and wanted to work the evening shift since her husband also worked that shift. She was pleasant and was more than qualified so she was hired on the spot.

All three were ready to work but would want three days to return to Dallas and collect their life's accumulation of 'stuff.' To their surprise all three were given a sign-on bonus of $250 and given a list of other employment benefits including a list of currently available apartments close to the hospital.

*

Meanwhile an event was happening that would affect the Duo's management of the Kelly Memorial Hospital for years to come.

Dumas Gregory entered the local Wells Fargo Bank and walked into President Rankin's office. "Mister Rankin, how much money do I have in your bank?" "Why at least a half million!" "Really, well if you want to keep it answer me one question. Do you hold the mortgage on the Kelly Memorial Hospital?" "No Sir!" "Ok, then I shall visit the Community National Bank but will have to transfer a part of this bank account to get them to answer my question, heh?" "Uh Sir, that won't be necessary. There is no mortgage on our hospital! It is no secret that Doctor Kelly used his inheritance to pay for the hospital's construction." "Really, well he must have taken the amount out of his bank account. How much was the final withdrawal?" "Uh, I cannot give you that info because of our privacy laws." Dumas turns to the office door and yells out, "cashier, please come in. I need to close my account!" "$50,000 and you never heard it from me!" "Amazing, then listen well, this is what I want you to do."

CHAPTER 9

Everyday Events

It was two weeks before Xmas and the Duo was talking in their parlor. Addie started, "everyone is talking about the dinner/dance we are planning at the Bluebird Dance Hall. It is clear that nurses and other workers like the idea of fraternizing between hospital employees, especially with the doctors—for it equalizes the hierarchy that exists. It is nice that single nurses get to dance with the eligible men such as JD, Frank, Reginald, and Angus while nurses also get to dance with the doctors to ease the formalities." "So it seems, well we will soon find out if the event is a success or a flop." "I also have been thinking, don't you think we should consider a monthly continuing education by the doctors presenting a topic that affects the nurses caring for our patients. For example, you are performing suprapubic prostatectomies and the nurses do not understand all the tubes you leave in these patients and the flushing instructions that are required." "Yes, you are right, and the less the nurses know what to do, the more our patients suffer. Let's plan on discussing this with the doctors at our monthly staff meetings and I will volunteer to do the first CME (continuing medical education) on prostatectomy care."

With Brad taking up a surgical magazine, Addie moved to their office to balance their bank book. With the monthly bank statement, she started the process. Suddenly, she walked out and sat by her husband and said, "I know how you hate to talk about money, but this is important. It appears that someone entered a $50,000 deposit into our account!" Brad cracked up and said, "why that is an error, we'll have to call President Rankin and make a correction, heh?" "Uh-uh I don't think so dear!" "Why?" "Because the deposit was made by Dumas Gregory! "Oh dear, now why did he do that?" "Probably because we accidentally saved his life and he is grateful, heh?" "Well a $500 donation would have been excessive in itself. Why pay off the hospital's construction bill?" "Who knows for sure, but a wealthy man does not need to ask anything in return. I still think he is a grateful man—nothing more, nothing less!" "Well time will tell! So what do we do with this unexpected windfall?" Addie thought it out and said, "we either set an amount aside for a future expansion or we see Angus and have a chat with him." "Why can't we do both?" "Ok, then we'll see Angus first thing in the morning."

Angus was still in the dining room enjoying his breakfast when the Duo came to his table. Shortly, they went to Angus's office. After explaining the windfall, Brad said that they would add another $10,000 to the account that Angus controlled to pay off the delinquent doctor and hospital bills. It was then Addie who said, "we thought you would make a list of the customers who pay a weekly or monthly payment that would take years to pay off their bills and pay off those bills. What do you think?"

Angus paused but finally said, "please do not ask me to do that, and let me explain why this is a bad idea. First of all I spend a lot of time checking out the people who currently get free care. In seven months I have used up $1,810 of that $5,000 fund. Here is the ledger that shows where every penny was spent. Now in this other ledger are the patients who pay anywhere from 10 cents a week to $1 a month. There are now 100 names. You would not believe the pride these patients have. They come to my half door, tap their dime on the door's platform and say, 'Jones here with #17 payment.' I accept the pay, enter their name and amount in the ledger. They then stand there till I drop the dime in the steel strongbox. These patients are so proud, we cannot take that away from them."

The Duo was stunned, speechless, and a bit embarrassed. Addie broke the ice as she said, "looking at the paid off debts thru the fund, what are these entries to the Merchasons?" "Well as I said, I carefully investigate the people that benefit from your fund. That often requires that I do a home visit. When I walk in, it is clear that the people are poor, their clothes are threadbare, kids walk barefoot, and everyone is 'skin on bones' on the edge of malnutrition. Yet the place is immaculate. Then I ask one clinching question. I ask a young kid, "what did you have for supper last night?" "Why we did not eat yesterday, it was our day off." "Well what did you have for breakfast today?" "A glass of milk from Susie our cow." "And what else are you getting for lunch?" "A pullet's egg from our chicken coop!" I often ask if the kids know what 'licorice' is. With a negative nod, I usually stop there, go see the Merchason market, pay off their credit bill, and take back to their home bags worth $20 of groceries. I cannot help it and I will gladly pay off those expenses out of my wages if you wish."

Brad had heard enough. Stood and said, "come Addie, it is clear that we chose the right man to do this job. Now Angus, the next time Addie and I come in here with another of 'our air-brain ideas,' kindly show us the door. You need to add $10,000 to the welfare account. And the next time you bring groceries back to the needy, make sure you bring a bag of licorice for the kids, and do something about shoes and clothing won't you. Just continue keeping a ledger of where you spend the money so we can look at it at the end of the year—at least bring it home overnight, heh?"

That night the Duo composed a careful letter to Mister Gregory expressing their appreciation for his generous gift. They also explained how they would use $10,000 to support their welfare account and $40,000 in a bank account for the next future expansion wing which would be called the Gregory Wing in his name.

*

The hospital party was a total success. The classic turkey meal was appreciated by all, everyone was well dressed in anything but hospital scrubs or uniforms, and everyone enjoyed the evening of dancing the Texas classic dances of the two-step and waltz. The talk throughout the evening was that hospital workers were accustomed to dinner and dancing at this club on Saturday evenings. Of course the doctors and their wives were all encouraged to join the festivities on their weekends off. It was no surprise that the Duo was first to join the club.

After the holidays things returned to normal. The greatest frustration that doctors faced in 1906 was the current treatment for cancer. It was a sad situation to admit that the accepted management included diagnose it, cut it out, radiate it, or treat it with laudanum. Diagnosis included a biopsy, an exploratory surgery, a blood test, or an X Ray. At that point it was hoped that it could be surgically removed. If not it was radiation in Dallas, or support to the end with laudanum. Every doctor knew there were no medicines available that could destroy cancer cells and would likely not be available for decades.

One day Trisha Camden showed up in the office with her husband. As Addie brought her from the waiting room, the two were reminiscing of happier days. When seated she asked Trisha the reason for their visit. "Two nights ago, Harold found a lump in my left breast, I cried for two days till this morning when I decided to do something about it." Brad listened to her story, obtained her family history, examined her, and then sat down to explain what his findings were and the current management that he and modern medicine could do for her.

"It is clear there is a lump in your breast that is suspicious for a malignancy. You also have an enlarged lymph node in your left armpit which is also suspicious. What I propose is that we do a pre-op chest X Ray and the usual pre-op blood tests. Tomorrow we will operate under chloroform anesthesia and remove the lump as well as that enlarged lymph node. We then wait while our pathologist, Doctor Greene, prepares the specimens, slices off thin samples, and examines them under the microscope. He will then walk his findings to the OR to tell the waiting Addie and me. If it is cancer in both specimens, we will perform a radical mastectomy to remove the breast and the underlying muscles that cancers tend to spread to. We will then close the chest wall with the reserved skin. Lastly, we will then explore your left armpit and remove all the dozen or so lymph nodes to be tested for cancer. After your surgical recovery and the analysis of the number of lymph nodes affected with cancer, we will send you to Dallas General for a month of daily external radiation treatments to destroy any residual cancer cells and hopefully prevent a recurrence of the disease." There was a long pause as Trisha finally asked, "this month-long treatment for radiation includes room and board." "Yes" "Can Harold and my two kids visit?" "Of course." "If I do not do this treatment, how long do I have to live?" "Possibly six months to a year." "If I go thru this disfiguring surgery and a month of radiation what are my survival chances?" "Current statistics show a five-year survival of 60%--which includes a cure diagnosis if you make it to 5 years."

Trisha dried a tear and said, "I have the most wonderful husband and kids, I have a lot of living to do, so I want everything you can do for me." Getting the nod from Harold, Trisha said, "let's do it!"

Over the year it seemed that more and more cancer cases were appearing. The surgeons had no choice with suspicious histories of abdominal symptoms than to perform exploratory abdominal laparotomies. The chest X Ray would easily identify lung cancer whereas the abdominal X Ray was not useful in detecting abdominal cancers. Unfortunately, so many laparotomies were an open and shut case from finding inoperable cancers. Either way, cancer treatment and diagnosis were still in the dark ages for medical doctors, but surgeons had the responsibility for saving as many victims as possible and carrying the drudge of providing bad news.

It would be five years when Trisha Camden would be given the coveted diagnosis of 'cured.'

*

1906 was a tumultuous year. It started with a bang when the night super called both surgeons, Doctor Greene, one nurse anesthetic, one OR nurse, and Addie to the EW. Addie recalls walking in with Brad as they saw a sight they would never forget. There was a young man with a 10-inch Bowie knife in his mid-right chest with the blade's tip protruding in the young man's back of his chest. The patient was on oxygen as Doc Greene was taking blood and starting an IV. Brad simply placed a sterile surgical glove over the blade's handle and said, "get this man to the OR." As the patient was being wheeled to the OR; Addie happened to see Dumas Gregory enter the EW as the patient was heard saying, "better pray for me Uncle Dumas!" Addie said nothing as she went to the nurses' changing room to get ready for surgery.

The operation started with a thoracotomy around the knife, once the rib spreader was applied, the knife was seen penetrating the middle of the 'right middle lobe' of the right lung. Brad never hesitated, he segregated the right main bronchus, vein, and artery and applied a total of six Kelly clamps. The knife was then pulled out and the right middle lobe was pulled out of the chest after cutting between the double Kelly clamps. After suturing off the artery, vein, and bronchus, a chest tube was left in place and connected to the air trapping bottle. The knife's penetration of the back of the chest was sutured and the front ribs reopposed with muscle, bone to bone, and skin sutures.

The two surgeons and Addie were in the recovery room when the young man's family were allowed a visit. There, stood Dumas Gregory and his sister Ida. Brad diplomatically said, "we had to remove 1/3 of his right lung, but if there is no infection, he should live a complete life with the lung he has left." Dumas never said a word—he had a smile and a shaking hand that said it all.

Once back home in bed Addie shocked Brad when she sat up and said, "I want a baby! This is still a savage land and we don't know if we will be alive tomorrow!" There was silence in the bedroom and Brad knew he had to be very careful and choose his words. Brad sat up and said, "there is probably no better time than now. We are trained, experienced, have a great bunch of professionals, and have a hospital in the black. I think you are right. However, I am somewhat spent after that harrowing case and maybe we could start working on that come morning, heh?" "Sure, but set the alarm an hour early so we can enjoy the event!"

In two months Addie was in the family way and then the avalanche started. Brad knew the gals were planning as there was plenty of 'girl talk' in the ladies' bathroom. Sally was next as Brad realized that the two nurse anesthetists would not be allowed to administer chloroform or ether in the first 16-20 weeks of pregnancy. So Brad contacted a 'locum-tenens' agency and hired two traveling nurse anesthetists that would be housed as roommates in a nearby apartment. One was a 50-year-old by the name of Etta Tyburski, and the other was a 45-year-old named Martha Tenoff. Everything worked out as both Ingrid and Marlene were with child by the time the relief nurse anesthetists arrived from Houston.

As the weeks progressed, all couples were with child. The ladies were all showing a 'bun' by April fool's day and a real 'belly' by the 4th of July. It was a hot summer and days of 100 degrees were common. The pregnant ladies all had a tough time but a surprise freight delivery raised some eyebrows There were five boxes each with an outside label—two for the operating rooms, one for the recovery room, one for the nurse and doctor lounges, and one for the EW. Inside each AC unit had an attached label that said, 'made especially for Dumas Gregory.'

Then another event seemed to compound the difficulty in maintaining fully operational staffing. The four single men had been stepping out with the large supply of young graduate nurses. By the fourth of July all four were married. Brad could foresee the future and all six apartments had to be converted from a single bedroom to two or three bedrooms. To make it worse, the time frame for renovations had to be stepped up when all four couples were in the family way.

Brad could not believe how everyone was putting safe sex aside and joining the band wagon even if summer was upon them. It was a necessary decision for nurses on break to cool down so a part of the recovery and EW were curtained off to allow nurses and staff to sit a spell in the air-conditioned rooms.

The closer to delivery, the more Brad saw future needs. To keep nursing moms working, they needed a place to nurse and care for their babies. Brad met with Mike who made it clear that there was no place for a nursery and a day care without adding a new wing. It was Addie who solved the problem. Addie asked Brad, "what are we planning for the extra two doctor offices/treatment rooms?" "Brad said, nothing for now, we actually have just the right number of doctors although Daniel and Stanley will be the next to get partners, but I think that is also a few years away." "Great, then why don't we move the furniture into storage and have Mike convert an office and treatment room into a nursery and the other into a daycare for toddlers—and hire a nanny for the nursery and daycare personnel when the time comes." "Done!"

It was a revelation to see all these very pregnant nurses and other workers walk around with their rotund bellies. The message was reaching the public and everyone would visit the hospital to see the parade of happy ladies.

As the pregnant gals were close to delivery, some went home for the last two weeks and some stayed on and would go into labor while working. Retrospectively, no one ever realized the stress these pregnant workers were placing on Doc and Missus Norwood. As hospital workers, there were no charges for obstetrical care, labor, delivery, and post- delivery care of mom and baby. Brad saw the dilemma and quickly authorized Angus to pay Doc Norwood's usual and customary fee for pregnancy care and delivery.

Addie was first to deliver and brought a 7-pound healthy boy into the world. Addie enjoyed her six weeks off to bond with her son. Brad also took a week off to spend with mom and baby, and then managed to hire the nursery nanny to care for Addie till she came back to work. One after the other, they delivered healthy babies as the post-delivery nursing nursery slowly filled up and the workers returned to full time employment as the 'locum-tenens' were discharged.

*

Thankful that nursing mothers rarely got pregnant while still nursing; there was a lull in pregnant ladies walking about the hospital. It was a regular workday when Missus Morse collapsed during office hours. The doctors all agreed that the cause of Missus Morse's persistent coma was because of a ruptured cerebral aneurysm and the prognosis was grave. Doc Morse had stayed at his wife's bedside for two days when the Doc felt a hand on his shoulders and the words, "Doc, why don't you step away and get some rest before you get sick. I will sit at her side and take care of her. I will especially give her the morphine IV doses she needs for sedation and comfort." Etta Tyburski never faulted. Except for quick trips to the bathroom she was steadfast at her responsibility. Even Doc Morse admitted that he appreciated the help from another person. It took another four days for Missus Morse to peacefully pass. Only then did Etta lay down to sleep. It was weeks later that Etta took on the job of being Doc Morse's office nurse. After six months of grieving, to no one's surprise, Doc and Etta were wed. After the honeymoon, Etta was again needed as a nurse anesthetist, as the gals were pregnant with their second child. The hospital provided Doc Morse an RN out of the nursing pool till Etta was free of anesthesia duty and able to return and work with her husband.

Yes, Addie was again pregnant. Brad was later quoted as saying, "thanks for natural birth control of nursing moms to space out the deliveries, heh?" History repeated itself and there was again a parade of round bellies. Despite the kids being in the daycare, the nurses and staff were able to continue performing their duties in the hospital.

Doc Norwood was in the Doctor's lounge one day and admitted that the worse thing about caring for hospital workers was the extra stress that came with each delivery. Of course he also admitted that delivering his wife Cindy had been the most stressful but most rewarding. Of course Doc Norwood never knew that Doc Morse had stood by in case Doc Norwood needed him, or that both surgeons and surgical staff stood by in case of an emergency C-Section.

During Addie's second pregnancy, Addie brought up an interesting point. "The ladies are all talking about getting a tubal-ligation after their second baby is born. Some want to wait and have one more, some are planning for the tubal right after delivery, and some want to wait at least three months to be sure the baby is healthy. We all know that as of today, this operation is not reversible. So what do you think about all this." "You know that I have a liberal philosophy about such things. What is important to me is what you want to do about this?"

Addie paused and finally said, "yes, I have done a lot of thinking about this, I lean on the side of caution but I am realistic. As for caution I think that waiting three months is wise. As far as reality is concerned, since I agreed to marry you and thereafter, I now find myself with three commitments: as my husband you are the first and I know that you have needs that safe sex does not satisfy. As the second are my children; I want to raise them and teach them values before they start school. As for my third commitment, it is the hospital. We are so busy with medicine, surgery, and administration that we do not have the time or energy or love to raise 6 to 8 kids. So as a compromise, if we have a healthy baby, then at three months, I will get a tubal before I get pregnant again. Can you go along with that?" "Absolutely and now I can stop worrying about doing a decent job as a father. I guess that's why I love you so."

As the second round of deliveries started there was a new twist as Addie had predicted. Every worker wanted a post-partum tubal-ligation either right away or within a few months. Doc Norwood was already working day and night, so he could not afford the time to perform the many requests for a surgical procedure while still in the post-delivery ward or months later. So both surgeons agreed to perform these operations in an alternating routine.

Although the patient and husband were well informed, both surgeons made it clear that the operation was a success 98% of the time and not reversible. This led to long discussions when the couple had two kids, but no discussion when a couple had over four kids or the couple was over 35 years of age. Months later, Addie gave birth to a healthy 6-pound 10-ounce girl. Three months later Tom performed her tubal- ligation.

*

By Xmas of 1907, Addie was back to work at least from 8AM to noon with the kids in the nursery and daycare. Certain changes were in the near future as the population of Amarillo was accelerating. By 1908 it was up to +-7,500. That is when Brad started planning an overall expansion to be completed by January of 1910 when the town's population was expected to reach 10,000. One night the Duo set up a tentative schedule of changes to include:

1. Addie resigned her assistant surgeon position and started half days doing administrative projects. Fortunately she had a reliable in-house nanny. It was a widowed grandmother who lived upstairs in her own apartment and would take care of the children during Addie's half days at the hospital.

2. Along with Addie's changes, Brad got into an arrangement with Dallas General to send a second-year resident to do an elective at the well- known Kelly Memorial Hospital. The first resident was Donald Scanlon MD, a single doc with special interest in fractures.

3. To coincide with the resident surgeon, Brad purchased a second apartment building near the first apartment building. Within a month another surgeon with a nurse anesthetist wife showed up from North Dakota. Damon Titus MD and wife Patricia were looking for a warmer climate This surgeon, trained at Dallas General, had two years' experience and an interest in gunshot wounds. The man and wife were hired as soon as their credentials and references were verified.

4. With a fourth surgeon Sally was able to resign as a surgical assistant and instead worked from home doing ledger entries and payroll for Angus.

5. With Doc Morse slowing down, Doc Reinhart needed help especially with the many tuberculosis cases in the local sanitorium. So Brad started advertising at the Dallas General Hospital and within a month a single graduating doctor, named Harold Tisdale

MD, took the job with special interests in tuberculosis.

6. To accommodate three new doctors, the doctor's wing was expanded and a total of five offices with a treatment room were added as well as the usual nursing nursery with a triple size daycare.

7. Other additions included one more OR nurse and a fulltime certified chest therapist.

8. The last change was to extend the Medical and Surgical wards by 25%--which could still be serviced by the existing ceiling utilities.

It was one of those bathtub meetings that Addie asked, "I hear that Ford is soon coming out with their Model T. When are we getting ours, it will be handy to get around with two kids?" "As soon as we both take driving lessons and I get several garages built for Doctor's Row and the two apartments, heh?" "Ok, and what else is new that I don't hear working in the administrative office." "Well we are adding two med/surg orderlies during the day shift and one during the evening in the ER. Oh I forgot to tell you but the Emergency Ward's name is now the Emergency Room (ER) since it is a room and not a ward."

There was a pause as Addie asked, "tell me what is new in the world of Internal Medicine." "Winston has taken a new approach with heart attack victims. No longer sedate and close the door. Now he is treating each patient with Nitroglycerin SL, IV morphine, Oxygen, and a new drug called procain which is a regional anesthetic that suppresses ventricular fibrillation and sudden death. Plus with all the nurses trained to do CPR he has added a pulse alarm, that is attached to a patient's forearm and when the pulse stops, a battery powered loud alarm sounds off. Of course the alarm is scaring the 'bi-Jees' out of the nearby patients especially when they see a nurse run in and they hear that darn 'precordial thump.'" "Sounds like we may soon need to modify a couple of rooms into an insulated separate unit that we can call an 'intensive care unit!'"

"Interesting, anything else?" "Yes, we are slowly getting new drugs. We have a first drug for syphilis called Salvarsan and a new oral pain killer called codeine which can be addicting but a lot better tasting than that awful laudanum." "Good, now tell me what is new about tuberculosis." TB can now be diagnosed by objective tests other than the history and clinical findings. Just to review, doctors used to use the history of fever, coughing up blood, fatigue, and weight loss. Today we add the clinical findings of moist 'rales' on chest auscultation, and we have a classic chest X Ray appearance. Now Doctor Greene can stain a patient's sputum and if he finds a gram-negative bacillus, then the diagnosis is locked up."

"Now explain to me why we send TB patients to the local sanitorium situated in the desert." "The city council uses property taxes to maintain a sanatorium so that we can pull tuberculous patients out of the family to avoid the family becoming infected. As it is a respiratory infectious process, we also need to take them out of the general population. Plus these patients need rest, cool dry air, and good nutrition, before serial improving chest X Rays can return these patients to their homes."

After another pause, Brad asked, "so what is new in administration?" "The state is working hard at finding ways to control everything we do. I fear the worse, but now enough talk, before the kids wake up, we'd better get to it, heh?"

*

Mike was busy with construction as other changes occurred as the building expansions were completed. Meanwhile, Brad and Addie were keeping up with national newspapers and the new radio broadcasts. It was clear that Europe was in the middle of a world war. France, England, and allies were trying hard to suppress the tyrant Germany and its allies. The US was so far kept out of the fracas but as a precaution general preparations were already starting as early as 1914.

To complicate the bad news of war, Europe was also dealing with a deadly infestation called the Spanish Flu which had a high mortality. Once the infection set in the trenches, more soldiers died of the flu than of bullets or bombs. The government leaders were certain that the US would be dragged into the war, as the medical society believed that the Spanish Flu would eventually reach the eastern US shores. If the US was getting ready for war, the medical communities were NOT getting ready to manage, educate, minimize, and treat a viral pandemic.

CHAPTER 10

1917 and Dealing with WWI

The years went by and the hospital flourished. Doctor Morse and Etta retired and moved to Fort Worth. The hospital was unchanged since the last changes were made in 1909. The staff was still the same except for the marriage of Doctor Scanlon and Mary Beers guaranteeing two essential positions. Doctor and Missus Titus had also become permanent fixtures although childless. The only recent addition was a new Obstetrician, Paul W Weiss MD and OR nurse wife Terry. The Doc specialized in gynecologic surgery, but would share the night and weekend call for deliveries. Doctor Greene never got a partner. Instead the hospital hired three certified laboratory technicians that were also certified in drawing blood and starting IVs. That left Doctor Greene with the more relaxed position of hospital pathologist and the new local medical examiner.

It was now January 1917 when Mayor Monroe came to see Doctor Kelly during his afternoon doing administrative duties with Addie. "So what brings you here Mayor?" "Well there are several events that may affect you and your hospital. We the city council feel that you should be present before decisions are made that may affect you but be too late to change." "Well under these conditions, I would like to arm myself with some help so if you tell me the issues, I will have the people there to give you answers or explanations." "In other words Doc, you don't want to walk into a gunfight with a hatchet in hand, heh?" "Yeah, something like that." "Then the subjects include the impending draft and dealing with the draft board, how the town should prepare for a pandemic of Spanish Flu, and further support of the TB sanatorium." "Wow, that means a long afternoon of meetings which we cannot afford the lost time. So make it an early evening meeting and I will have with me the appropriate people who can provide authoritative answers." "Fair enough, how about this week on Friday evening at 6PM?" "Done."

The meeting was held in the mayor's conference room. Mayor Monroe welcomed all the parties involved including the Kellys and their entourage. "Have a seat folks and I will introduce all the parties involved. To my right is the Amarillo and Potter County draft board that consists of Judge Gagnon as head chair and the other members that include Frank Tisdale, Merton Merchason, Sheriff Butler, and President Homer Rankin. Note the five members so any vote will not be a tie vote. To my left is the city council. Note the white hair as the council is made up of the so called 'town fathers.' Also dispersed around are invited dignitaries to include Lt. Col. Armand G. Lee, Dumas Gregory city philanthropist, Artemis Goodson RR station manager, Luke Carson Amarillo Sanatorium general manager, and the Texas State Health Commissioner William Hallett MD."

After introductions, Brad said, " you all know my wife Addie and this is JD Sinclair our purchasing agent, Mary Scanlon RN nursing supervisor, and Doctor Tom Hall, general surgeon." "Very good, now I will have the groups' leaders explain why they called this meeting."

Judge Gagnon. "We are here to represent the Federal government's war effort. If the US enters the war in Europe, the draft will be enacted and will include any able-bodied man between the ages of 21 to 31 years of age. Right now the only exceptions are those who have a medical disability or are employed in manufacturing war supplies and arms. We are not here to cripple your hospital for it is also our hospital. But we are hoping to get voluntary enlistments to include three RNs and one surgical doctor, or more if volunteerism is patriotic." If we do not get our quota we cannot draft female nurses, but we can draft male doctors."

Lt. Col. Lee. "I am the US Army recruiter. I am here to register the names of anyone enlisting voluntarily— nothing more, nothing less!"

Murdock Hatfield. "I am the current president of the Amarillo city council. Let it be known that this council strongly supports the Kelly Hospital and its doctors. Plus we are here to help protect the quality care we have received for the past 12 years."

Mayor Monroe then moved to start the negotiating process. "Doctor Kelly would you elucidate who you have on staff that may qualify for inscription into the US Army and give us your minimal staffing to continue your present care level." "Certainly, my wife Adelle, co-owner of the Kelly Hospital and general administrator will answer those questions. Addie ... " " We have four ancillary workers and three doctors less than 31 years of age. With 12 years of experience, it is now very clear that Kelly Hospital needs the four ancillary positions filled at all times. Plus Internal Medicine doctors and three surgical doctors must be kept on staff to serve the +- 15,000 inhabitants in Amarillo. Keep in mind that our two medical doctors will be needed in planning our pandemic defenses as they will also be the leading doctors in caring and treating the influenza victims."

Next to address the draft board was JD Sinclair. "Sirs, I am the purchasing agent and have been so for 12 years. I am married with two children. I speak representing the three other ancillary workers: pharmacy, accounting, and X Ray technology. We will not be enlisting because of the chaos our absence will cause to the Kellys and all of the hospital workers. However if we are drafted, we will all proudly serve the US Army Medical Corps."

Judge Gagnon interrupted. "Doctor Kelly, is that true?" "Yes Sir any hospital cannot function without those four positions being filled with competent workers. I admit that it is the position that is crucial and not the people working the department for we are all replaceable, heh?"

There was a pause as Judge Gagnon said, "if we draft them, how will you manage?" "I would be on the telegraph negotiating for expensive replacements thru a private 'locum-tenens' agency." "Please explain." "A locum-tenens agency is a private enterprise that keeps trained medical personnel as their employees. For someone like me, I will aggressively be a bidder to win the prize of paying that agency a ridiculous highway robbery fee to just have the honor of that employee joining us at three to four times usual and customary wages. As the saying goes, that is the nature of the beast!"

Judge Gagnon looked at his other board members who were all shaking their heads negatively. "Doctor Kelly, we will not do that to you. Besides, by the time these four essential workers were drafted and processed, they would all four be over the age of 31 anyways. No, let's move on."

Brad then nodded to Mary who stood up. "My name is Mary Scanlon RN, and I am the nursing supervisor at Kelly Memorial. I can attest to the fact that I have spoken to every nurse working at the hospital. I am pleased to announce that four RNs have assured me that if the US enters the war against Germany, that they would all immediately enlist in the medical nursing corps. Two would request a field hospital on the front, and two would request a base hospital." The Lt. Col. stood and said, "thank you and I will get their names after the meeting."

Brad then asked Doctor Hall to take over. "I am here as a senior surgeon to represent the three new doctors under 31 years of age. The one Internal Medicine and two general surgeons have never been militarily inclined. I have spoken to all three and not one will enlist if we go to war. However, if drafted they will proudly serve the US Army and our USA." A hand went up as the mayor acknowledged the applicant.

"My name is Luke Carson, general manager of the Amarillo Sanatorium. I am requesting an exemption for Doctor Tisdale. Since his arrival he has been a Godsend for our sanatorium. We are running full occupancy with 30 resident patients. With Doctor Tisdale's careful evaluations, we now have patients coming to the hospital for chest drainage surgery, and we also have discharges to home which now allows us to accept new patients—patients from our community I remind you. Plus, Doctor Tisdale comes regularly to our office and follows up on those discharge patients with clinical exams and X Rays. In short we need him and so do you. Remember, not every doctor will take the risk and willingly treat TB patients."

Judge Gagnon asked, "Missus Kelly, of these three doctors are they married and do they have children?" "They are all three married and their wives are specialized nurses that work for our hospital. There are no children as of yet." "And as the head administrator, do you agree that Doctor Tisdale will be essential in designing a defense against this epidemic?" "Yes!"

Feeling that an end was near, Judge Gagnon added, "well Doctor Kelly, if war comes and the draft is enacted, we will notify you of our decision. Thank you for coming and for your honesty and dedication to our community." Suddenly a hand went up.

"Excuse me, but before we leave this meeting, didn't you say you wanted three RNs and one doctor? Well by my count you have four RNs and one doctor. So let's put this draft threat to bed, heh?" "But Doctor Hall what part of tonight's discussion did we get wrong?" Tom gets Brad nod as he says, "gentlemen, if the US enters the war against Germany and enacts the draft I will voluntarily enlist and ask for an assignment in a field hospital." Addie just about fell off her chair as she looked at Brad as if to say, "where does that come from, or wait till I get your home dear husband."

There not being any further points to rehash, Mayor Monroe then moved the subject matter to the predicted Influenza pandemic. "We are all very anxious to know how our town can prepare for a viral epidemic that can devastate our community—knowing that there are no antiviral medicines to kill this scourge."

Doctor Kelly. "As we speak, our hospital is at 100% occupancy. Were we presently facing the pandemic, we could not even admit one severely ill patient with influenza—unless we put them on the floor in the receiving central square. So to care for influenza patients in the next six months, we need to start building a new wing today. Were we to build a 250 by 30-foot wing with several five bed wards we could house 50 patients at one time."

Mayor Monroe. "But Doctor Kelly if we go with predicted statistics, we expect 20% or our 15,000 inhabitants to get the flu. That amounts to 3,000 influenza victims of which at least 10% will be sick enough to not be cared for at home. That amounts to 300 hospitalized patients of which many will have the more serious complication of pneumonia."

Addie. "That is true. But don't forget that those 300 victims will not all get sick the same day. Admissions will be in waves of infected locations in town. What we propose is to have an attached 'rented hospital tent' for the patients who have improved and need less medical care than the ones in the new hospital wing."

Mayor Monroe. "I can see your point, but don't you think it would be wiser to have two wings and handle 100 sick patients at one time?"

Doctor Kelly. "The answer is no and for three reasons. First the building cost to erect a 7500 square foot building in 1917 is +-$3 a square foot or +-$25,000, and to fill it with beds, equipment and the complicated utilities is another $15,000 or a total of +-$40,000. We have the reserved funds to build one wing, not two. Secondly, where are we going to get the nursing staff, orderlies, chest therapists, and add to our kitchen and cooks to man this new wing. There is a graduating class of nurses this August from Dallas. We can attract many of these nurses but that means guaranteeing a salary months before they are needed. We can handle one such batch of preemptive employments but not two. Thirdly, once the pandemic is over what are we to do with the two new wings. We can certainly use one up to expand our hospital over the next five years. But not two extra wings. One will become a 'white elephant.' No thanks, we will build one wing but not two—and that's a deal breaker."

Mayor Monroe. "Even if we paid for the second wing."

Addie. "It is not just the money but the other two reasons as well. Better still, put your surplus of tax payments to better use and continue funding the Amarillo Sanatorium or open a town nursing home which is so much needed!" Feeling overwhelmed, the mayor asked, "Mister Gregory how do you feel about this?"

Dumas Gregory. "I am in total support of the Kellys point of view. No one wants to waste hard earned dollars on a white elephant. Besides, I see nothing wrong for convalescing influenza victims to be recovering in a 'rented hospital tent.'" "And Mister Goodson what are your thoughts on this subject?"

Artemis Goodson. "The railroad employees have enjoyed quality health care for years. If the Kellys feel that one new wing will do the job, I am certainly going to agree with the local experts, heh?" "Ok, and Doctor Hallet what are your thoughts on this matter?"

Doctor Hallett. "The Kellys have impressed me that they have very sound judgement. Go with them. From medical enlistments to preparing for a pandemic, I fear not all communities of this size will be so patriotic or ready to deal with a killing pandemic. You are all so fortunate."

*

Mike Walters saw the need to start placing orders for construction and medical supplies. Anticipating a world war meant a total stoppage in construction and medical paraphernalia; he spent a complete week to order every possible item needed to erect, support with utilities, add beds and a myriad of items. Fortunately he had kept the records from the 1905 construction and setting up of each room. These records were very helpful in guiding the salesmen in supplying what was needed. To hold all these purchases, his own warehouse would be used for storage till the items were needed. Meanwhile his carpenters were setting a concrete footing and pouring a concrete floor before the brick layers went to work.

It was April when several freight and cruise ships were sunk by German U-boats. President Wilson went to Congress and got permission to declare war on Germany and its allies. The war effort accelerated and American soldiers were sent to the front. With the addition of field hospitals to treat the injured, Tom's promise to the local draft board came to fruition.

*

Meanwhile Doc Hall was in the recruiter's office. Lt. Col. Lee explained that doctors would be given the rank of captain and would spend a couple weeks of so called 'basic training' for doctors. This was not an exercise and learning to kill program, but learning military etiquette and the style that officers were expected to represent. After their basic training, the doctors were assigned their official uniforms, shown the standard layout of a field hospital, and scheduled to board a freighter loaded with artillery, artillery shells, small arms, ammunition and hundreds of doctors, nurses, and orderlies. With all this precious cargo, that ship was escorted with two submarines and two surface destroyers well-armed with depth charges. It took two weeks for a ship from Galveston, Texas to arrive in France.

The two weeks were used to prepare the enlisted surgeons. The bulk of the surgeons came from Brooke Medical Center of Fort Sam Houston in San Antonio. With a renown trauma and research center, they supplied a large portion of field hospital surgeons.

While heading to France, Tom recalled the obligatory classes for enlisted non-military career doctors.

"Good day, I am Colonel MH Stanhope MD. I will discuss the reason a field hospital can save so many lives. Remember our moto; 'FIX IT QUICK OR REMOVE IT.' Let me explain. Would you prefer to save one soldier and let 9 die in the pre-op ward; or save 7-9 out of ten. That is currently our record in Asian wars. The triage nurse will separate the ones we can save and present each soldier in the degree of severity and emergency. The triage nurse will unfortunately segregate the ones that are beyond our technical know-how—which is usually the head injuries unless we are lucky to have a neurosurgeon on our staff."

"So you wonder how this can be done while hoping your operating room will not be hit with a wild artillery explosion since most field hospitals are within 200-300 yards of the American trenches. Well it is all a matter of choosing the right procedure that will save hours and save most of the waiting soldiers. Take a gunshot to the right upper chest. The rifles used are high velocity and the damage done to a lobe of lung is unimaginable. To repair it will take three hours with severe blood loss which will utilize our poor blood supply and reels of catgut/chromic catgut we do not have. Then to make it worse, the incidence of infection, bleeding, and air leaking will then require a repeat operation to do what should have been done the first time. NOW WHAT IS WRONG WITH THIS PICTURE. An emergency lobectomy done by two surgeons can take 15 MINUTES. Can anyone justify saving a lobe of lung and losing a bunch of waiting soldiers on the edge of death?"

"The procedure that should have been done is a right upper lobectomy—getting immediate hemostasis, clamp off the right upper bronchus, artery, and vein and pull the upper lobe out with quick blunt dissection. Close the chest and stand back as the patient is rolled off your OR table. The next anesthetized soldier is placed on the table while you stand there with your unchanged glove and gown— with rinsed gloves if sterile water or saline is available."

There was plenty of reflection as the colonel continued. "The worse situation with trench warfare is for a trench being overrun by enemies using their close-range bayonets. You will see plenty of bayonet wounds to the chest and will be tempted to sew up a lacerated lobe. Do not consider it if there is active fighting. Yet if there was a lull in fighting and a single chest bayonet wound appeared; this is the time to try to save a lobe. It will be a slow meticulous repair of cut arteries, veins, and bronchioles, but it can be done."

"Next, let's talk about abdominal wounds. Whether it is by gunshot, bayonet, or shrapnel it requires precious time. Even using X Rays to find the shrapnel or bullet, you not only need to oversew all holes, you need to run the entire bowel from stomach to rectum—and hope you don't have to add a second procedure to form an ileostomy or colostomy, heh?" So don't be surprised if the triage officer places these cases at the end of the line and keeps them well sedated with morphine!"

"The most painful subject for me to discuss is the trauma caused by artillery and its resultant need for amputations . It is a clinical decision to make. Can a leg or arm be saved with reasonable surgery time and the minimal chance of infection without amputation. Years ago we knew that a careful amputation took one to two hours. Now with the use of a new instrument called the 'guillotine,' two surgeons can do an amputation in a half hour. A decision needs to include the degree of damage, especially to nerves or arteries, the number of waiting cases, and the estimated time to save that soldier/s leg. One day you will all become the senior surgeon and you will be the one to make that life and death decision. For the beginning months, your surgical partner will be the senior surgeon and will make those decisions."

The remainder of the days were spent reviewing the actual procedures to be performed in a field hospital. Several days were spent on repairing arteries, bronchioles, tendons, and intestines and with the specific chosen sutures if available.

The mainstay of general intra-operative and post-op care was IV's and oxygen since blood for blood type specific transfusions was difficult to come by. The standard IV for shock and surgery was normal saline. The maintenance IV included sugar (dextrose) and potassium added to half-strength saline to make a D5W ½ saline with 20 milli-equivalents of potassium. Maintaining a sustenance nutrition was difficult on the front when MREs were the only available source of food. The other shortage was sterile bandages and often minimally stained dressings were reused.

After weeks on the ocean, they arrived in France. Without wasting time they were all farmed out to different field or base hospitals. Tom recalled years later his first conversation with the field hospital officer in charge—Colonel Samsom B Whittemore MD.

"Well what have we here, an enlisted volunteer general surgeon with a dozen years' experience. Why on earth would you leave a money- making surgical career to volunteer for a dangerous position on the front?" "Well Sir, I feel I was fortunate to have 12 productive years in Texas, and now is the time to do my part and hopefully learn the new military ways so I can bring back some of those lifesaving procedures." "I see, so you have had experience with gunshots and knife wounds?" "Yes Sir, Texas is still a violent land and cowboys like to settle things with their guns and knives. Although my past experiences will not come into play. I am well aware of the need for surgical expediency in face of active fighting. I am more than willing to work with any senior military surgeon as I will learn by doing." "I have heard enough Captain Hall, have a seat and I will get you a senior surgeon."

"Captain Tom Hall MD of Amarillo, Texas, this is Lt. Col. Chester Butler MD. Assistant professor of surgery in the Trauma Center at Brooke Medical Center. He has 20 years of service and at least experience in one Asian war. You will be his assistant surgeon until you earn your way to become a senior surgeon. Thank you for your service and pray that you do not get injured from a wayward artillery bomb."

The two surgeons spent time getting acquainted while sitting in the officers' quarters when the sirens sounded of impending casualties. Tom was escorted to the operating theatre. Doctor Butler said, "scrub well because you may only have one chance to do so." Stepping in the OR, he saw six OR tables ready to receive the wounded. Once triaged and prepped with iodine, oxygen, IV, and some already under anesthesia, the bodies arrived on the tables.

The Butler/Hall team's first case was a presumed rifle shot to the right chest. With a 10-inch thoracostomy incision in the lower chest, the rib separator was set. The right lower lobe was mush. Doctor Butler never hesitated as he clamped the RLL trunk of artery, bronchus, and veins. Tom got a firsthand experience in removing the lobe. When Doc Butler said, "that does it, let's close up, leave an air trapping bottle, and move on to the next case." To his surprise, Tom said, "we aren't done doc. We have a tear in the diaphragm and as there is no bullet exit wound, we likely have shrapnel in the liver."

The diaphragm rent was extended and the shrapnel was quickly found. After suturing the liver with O-chromic, the diaphragm was repaired and the chest rib/intercostals were quickly sutured. With an air trapping bottle in place, the team moved over to a macerated lower leg. There was no doubt as Doc Butler prepared the guillotine. With it set, he pressed the release and Tom nearly collapsed. Doc Butler said, "sorry Tom there was no preparing you, for it is the nature of the beast. Tie off the bleeders and let's close skin flaps to make a stump as we move to the next soldier waiting, heh?"

One after the other, devastating injuries were the norm. That day they performed two emergency splenectomies, a nephrectomy, and several liver shrapnel wounds. Fortunately intestinal lacerations and bullet holes were rare, but at the end of fighting, a man to man fighting yielded bayonet punctures to every part of the upper torso. The one injury that Tom had not expected was shrapnel injuries to the face. Because there were no plastic surgeons on the front line, the general surgeons had to use a lot of 4-O and 5-0 silk to repair the disfiguring lacerations. Usually these injuries were last to be repaired and kept moist with saline dressings till the surgeons were available.

The first round of surgery to handle all the wounded soldiers lasted ten hours. Afterwards, instead of getting some sleep, Tom would step into the neurosurgical ward and help the surgeons do 'Burr holes' to evacuate epidural hematomas, or open a skull to reach bleeding brain tissues. Tom became adept in cutting out a skull flap that could be reused to close the surgical window, and learned several techniques in repairing damaged brain tissue from trauma—especially gunshots.

Weeks went by as he and Sally would write twice a week since many letters never made it across the ocean. Tom had been Doc Butler's assistant for eight weeks when Tom graduated to senior surgeons and was given an enlisted surgeon from Houston Texas of all places—but with only one years' experience doing elective surgery and no experience in trauma.

Despite teaching the military ways of trauma surgery, Tom still assisted other surgeons to learn fine vascular and nerve repairs, as well as the proper management of shattered and exposed fractured bones. The open memorable operation was a bullet wound to the neck with a pulsating carotid artery. The vascular surgeon took over and showed Tom how to add a diverting rubber tube and safely clamp off the carotid to do a fancy carotid artery repair with 5-0 monofilament non-absorbable sutures.

It was November when Tom was offered the position of head surgeon in the field hospital. Tom proudly accepted and after a week, the war came to an end. When he was asked if he would transfer to a base hospital to continue caring for soldiers, he said, "no. My life and ties are with my wife, kids, my hospital, and doctors that made me the man I am. I have done my duty and I am heading back home."

*

Meanwhile life in Amarillo and the Kelly Memorial Hospital had changed during the war. With all the young men gone to war, women had taken over manufacturing jobs. There was no money in town and so people were not walking about. The hospital continued to provide services but there was no elective surgery being done. All surgery came from the ER and included fractures, shootings, trauma, and the common infections such as appendicitis, diverticulitis, and cholecystitis Brad later realized that many other changes occurred to include:

1. The hospital census crashed with the absence of elective surgery. Plus more medical conditions were being treated at home since people did not have the extra money to cover hospital bills.

2. Several RNs had to be sent home each day but at full pay.

3. Tubal-ligations were put on hold unless it was a family with 5 or more healthy children. Mothers with 2-3 kids would hold off getting sterilized especially if their husbands were off to war. Also important was the fear of dealing with influenza when it was known to be deadly to newborns up to 2 years-of-age children.

4. With men at war there was no money coming in. So pregnant gals would admit that they could not pay their delivery fees.

5. Food was short and pregnant gals had trouble maintaining a balanced diet for proper

nutrition—for both mom and baby. It was such a case that represented many of the obstetricians' patients.

A pregnant lady admitted to Cindy Norwood that with five kids, they could not pay for her obstetrical care or the tubal-ligation planned after the birth. Knowing the family situation, Cindy brought the couple to see Angus McKenzie in accounting. Angus questioned them and listened to the husband's story. "We are homesteaders living off the land. Our corn crop failed last year because of drought. So meeker savings disappeared and now money is gone. We have a large overdue credit at Merchasons but they are not pushing us. Yet we try to live off the garden and chicken coop. So food is scarce. Despite all this, we borrowed money from the bank and purchased new equipment with a delayed payment at harvest time.

We have three crops growing and if there is enough rain we will have a cash crop of sugar beets, and commercial crops of corn and turnips.

Angus listened attentively and then asked, "who is thinning out the sugar beets and cultivating the other vegetables?" "Why me and my five kids do all the work while school is out." "Do your kids have shoes?" "Yes but only for school and church." After more personal questions Angus realized that an intervention was absolutely needed.

Angus started, "it is obvious that you were once financially stable but because of drought, you are now in trouble and it is time for you to 'get a break.' I am happy to tell you that we have a Benefactor Fund set up by an anonymous doner. We will use that fund and pay all your obstetrical, tubal-ligation, hospital, and all doctor bills. Plus we will pay off your grocery credit bill and leave you a credit of $25. Here is $25 in cash to buy current groceries. There is more, buy your kids new work shoes and work clothing. You Sir, you need new work clothes and you Ma'am, you need three maternity outfits. Plus make sure you get five bags of candy for your kids. We do this under one condition, that you eat properly and give us a good baby, heh? I will contact the Merchasons and will arrange for the payment of your account by the Benefactor Fund."

*

Throughout the war months, Mike did well to build the new 'flu wing.' Erecting the brick shell went smoothly, but doing the 'finish\ work with all the utilities took several months. To everyone's surprise the 'flu wing' would be ready for occupancy by the time the holidays arrived.

As the summer had progressed the two medical doctors were busy getting the locals ready to think along the lines of surviving a pandemic. Each week they would write a column in the local newspaper on how to get ready to deal with a pandemic. The early columns covered planting large gardens and put away food by canning. Then came articles on frugality and avoiding frivolous expenditures during hard times. Eventually the columns covered prevention by avoiding large crowds and never leaving home without a face mask. Things started to get real when the docs mentioned, as the cases were rising, that the mayor would shut down the town. All businesses would be closed, the railroad would only handle freight, and the only business left open would be the grocers, butchers, pharmacies, and necessary medical care thru the hospital ER. To impress the readers. The docs predicted that with a town population of 15,000 that they should expect 3,000 cases of flu of which 300 would be sick enough to end up in the hospital and likely for pneumonia.

The totally unanticipated supply problem was that commercial IV fluids were not available because they had been transferred to the war front lines. Frank Libby decided to make his own. He would boil water in the kitchen, add Dextrose, salt, or half salt with or without potassium to make Normal Saline or D5W ½ saline, with or without 20 milliequivalents of potassium. Since empty bottles were easily available, he prepared during six weeks, large stores of ready IV fluids for maintaining hydration, electrolytes, nutrition, and treatment for shock.

During the summer, the entire old and new nursing staff were trained to do proper chest percussive therapy in the treatment of the deadly complication—pneumonia. Other preparations included precautions for each nurse to never enter the hospital without a face mask as the breathing droplets were known to cause the infection transfer to other people. The nurses also learned how to deal with many complications of the flu to include fever, diarrhea, vomiting, general pain, and maintaining nutrition and hydration or resorting to IV fluids.

The hospital also purchased a portable X Ray unit to obtain bedside serial chest X Rays to follow pneumonia victims. The pharmacy loaded up with the standard medicines used from day to day and especially the ones that would be used in the 'flu wing.'

The late item was erecting the rented hospital tent. It was early especially since it would be used for convalescing flu victims, but to be assured it would be available, it was erected just before Xmas.

With the addition of more cooks and new commercial cooking and refrigeration units, the kitchen staff was ready. Without doubt, by Xmas the hospital was ready for 1918 and the expected pandemic.

CHAPTER 11

The 1918 Influenza

Tom had notified Sally after the war ended that he was coming home. Sally was so happy and scared that she cried every day for a month. The kids now ages 7, 9, and 11 were so happy to see dad come home that they could not go to school till they saw the man for themselves. It was two days before Xmas when the train from Galveston arrived with soldiers coming home. In the crowd was Captain Hall. Although most of the hospital staff had gathered to meet their surgeon, the family was allowed a private meeting with their husband and father. Once the crying stopped, the entire platform of medical workers swarmed to welcome their favorite son back.

It was at that moment that the Duo had an epiphany. The rail platform of soldiers was revealing. Brad said to Addie, "how many of those soldiers have the flu but said nothing. This is what will bring the flu to all parts of the west and eastern portions of the country." Addie added, "then I suspect that by mid-January we will begin to see the early cases."

Mayor Monroe was getting reports from major employers of daily absences from work because of the flu, but relied more on the hospital census in the flu ward. Doc Kelly recalls the sequence of daily census changes. January 21 two cases with severe dehydration. January 22 the first case of pneumonia. January 23 three more very sick cases. January 24 a total of six cases, two of which were bad pneumonia cases. January 25 Mayor Monroe shut down the town. Two days later the mayor was admitted with bilateral pneumonia and in an acute extremis state. The cases then flowed in regularly, and sometimes exponentially, till the flu wing was up to maximum occupancy—50 deathly ill patients by February 15th.

It was while spending a rare evening at home during the shutdown that Addie answered Brad' s question, "now that we have a full house, how does the schedule look like to take care of these patients?" "Well I could say that we are using every able person we have but I will be more specific. First of all everyone works either an eight-hour shift or a twelve- hour shift, and seven days a week. The staff layout and numbers are as follows:

RNs

WARD NURSES—25, OR nurses—2, Nursing and OR supervisors—2, Night supers—3, Doctors nurse/wives—5. A total of 37 but minus 3 for the ER and 3 for post-op surgical care 24-hour coverage. Leaving a total of 31 assigned to the flu ward.

SURGEONS. Four are each assigned on a 6-hour shift around the clock for chest tube insertion and other procedures (see surgical care).

MEDICAL DOCTORS. Two are assigned to each a 12-hour shift.

ORDERLIES. Two are assigned to each a 12-hour shift.

ANCILLARY STAFF. Four as usual assigned an 8-hour day shift but on call 24 hours a day.

DOCTOR GREENE. On 8-hour day shift but on call 24 hours a day.

KITCHEN. Three on 8-hour shifts.

HOUSEKEEPERS. Four—two on days, one on evenings, and one on nights.

VOLUNTEERS. Eight—four on days, two on evenings, and two on nights.

EXCLUSIONS. Anyone working in the maternity ward is excluded and actually not even allowed to enter the flu ward—that includes doctors and nurses. Actually only the fathers can enter but must stay in the mom's rooms until mom and baby are discharged."

"Now in my book that comes to +- 50 active providers and 8 volunteers spread over three shifts to care for 50 active influenza patients, up to 40 recovering patients, an unknown number of post-op patients, and a fluctuating number of patients coming thru the ER."

"That brings up the issue whether we should close the hospital to visitors.?" "As the presiding administrator, I have already done so. Visitors, except for a next of kin, are not allowed entry during the pandemic. One such named person can enter the flu ward at their own risk. Each visitor is required to wear a face mask and spend a maximum of 15 minutes with their loved one to carry a family message or to take care of the patient's business matters. Now as the medical director, what are you requiring of all admissions?"

"Each admission will have a CBC (blood count), and chemistries to include electrolytes, glucose, renal, and liver functions—obviously to check for anemia, diabetes, dehydration, hepatitis, or actual liver and renal failure. If there are any respiratory symptoms, such as a cough or shortness of breath, a baseline chest X Ray will be done. Nearest of kin will be recorded with you and with the welcome counter. Sputum will be collected for Doc Greene to analyze; to differentiate bacterial versus a viral infection. Then other than getting a careful history of the present illness, past illnesses, and a complete physical exam; the patient will have an IV started and placed on oxygen if indicated. After the patient is assigned a nurse, further treatments will be provided as needed."

Addie was curious about routines and asked, "let's take a sick patient that is dehydrated and has pneumonia. Other than the admitting process, what will be the patient's 'day to day' routine?" "You mean like what Mayor Monroe went thru?" "Yes!" "Follow this routine:

- Documentation of patient's resuscitation status.
- Vital signs every four hours.
- I & O documented (intake and output).
- Serial daily chest X Rays and blood chemistries.
- Doctor visits every six hours.
- EKG for any irregular pulse (see medical care).
- Appropriate treatment for associated symptoms.

- Bedtime small dosage of morphine to enable restful sleep.
- Chest percussive therapy. As the IV is curative for dehydration, so is chest PT for pneumonia. Each patient will receive 15 minutes each hour from 6AM to Midnight, one at 3AM, and using two positions downward—face down and affected chest side up.
- Every patient gets the usual general nursing care."

"Speaking of medical care, let's go over the major issues that complicates a patient's hospital course." "Ok, but I will save the worst one for last.

1. Shock. Some patients arrive so dehydrated, that like the Mayor, an IV of saline had to be started and given a full volume load to regain a normal blood pressure.
2. Dehydration causes must be controlled. Nausea treated with plant based anti-emetics, and diarrhea treated with codeine or bismuth.

3. Renal failure. Dehydration will raise the BUN but not the creatinine and it is generally reversible with hydration.

4. Liver failure. An associated secondary viral hepatitis is common with or without liver failure but is also generally reversible as the illness resolves.

5. Inspissated bronchial secretions (dry and thick) must be loosened with the 'super saturated solution of potassium iodide' (SSKI). Required for chest percussive therapy to be effective.

6. Stroke. This is commonly seen with patients arriving in an extremis condition. Unfortunately the treatment is supportive.

7. Other common symptoms include: morphine for muscle pain, aspirin for fever, oxygen for hypoxia, codeine elixir for a nuisance cough, and antacids for reflux and gastritis.

8. Carditis and its varied presentation of CHF, Angina, cardiac arrest and other arrythmias. Whether it is caused by the stress of the illness or a direct infection of the heart structure

is not yet known. CHF. May be transient or permanent and is treated with Digitalis, injectable mercurial diuretics, salt restriction, intermittent epinephrine injections, and oxygen.

ANGINA. It is common for this complication to appear during an influenza infection. The treatment is also oxygen and sub lingual nitroglycerine. Sometimes it is a true heart attack and not angina.

CARDIAC ARREST. If the patient has an irregular pulse and proven to have PVCs on EKG; then the risk of a sudden ventricular fibrillation will lead to cardiac arrest. Like a heart attack, those patients are prophylactically placed on procain and aspirin.

OTHER ARRYTHMIAS. Atrial fibrillation is commonly seen in patients older than 50 and is treated with digitalis."

"Why that was a nice review, now tell me what surgical care involves." "Surgical care of influenza victims is anticipatory. If a patient has pneumonia and has a pleural effusion, empyema, or a pneumothorax, then a chest tube to suction is needed. Similarly if a patient has severe CHF with pleural effusion that worsen hypoxia, then a chest tube is indicated. Once a chest tube is in, the surgeon must watch the suction bottle to be sure it is functioning properly. Plus chest X Rays must be done serially. Unfortunately these patients also suffer from gangrene of fingers or toes from low blood oxygen levels (hypoxia) and need amputations to control infections. Plus on each shift, the surgeons check patients' chest for clinical signs of fluid accumulation and the need for chest tubes."

Addie felt reassured that the organization and the many devoted workers would get the bulk of the patients thru this scourge.

*

Despite the best laid out plans, a patient arrived one day that did not fit in the system. Addie was the flu wing unit clerk in charge of admissions. The look of the patient in the wheelchair shocked Addie. "Hello Miss Truax, you don't look well." "After years of fighting diabetes, I am afraid that this influenza has the best of me." "Well let's have the doctor evaluate you and we'll go from there."

After her blood tests and X Rays, Addie was visiting and enjoying the nostalgia of reliving her days in high school. Miss Truax said, "I still remember you sitting in my science class. I was so glad to hear that you sold the ranch and went to nursing school Now you are co-owner of this hospital and a surgical assistant. Good for you!"

Doctor Kelly came to sit with Addie and Miss Truax, "well Doctor, give it to me straight!" "You have an extensive pneumonia in both lungs and a large amount of chest fluid on both sides. Plus you have a blood sugar above 700 and you are going into ketoacidosis. That will lead to coma and you know there is no treatment for diabetes. Plus you need chest tubes in each chest and that is rather painful just to have one, to say the least." "That is Ok doc. I knew that my time had come. It is just that I am alone in this world and I do not want to die alone. I admit that I am afraid of dying, so can you help me controlling

my anxiety?" "We can do that!" "And can you keep
me sleeping at the end—dying in my sleep has always
been my wish as long as someone is with me." "Addie
will sit with you, administer morphine when needed,
and be with you till the end."

It was a 24-hour vigil as Addie administered
morphine to keep her patient sedated and free of
anxiety. When the time came, she passed in her
sleep. To this day, Addie still believes that Miss Truax
touched her cheek as the window curtains swayed
back and forth as she passed to the other side.

It was of note that Mayor Monroe responded
well to hydration and chest therapy. Without further
complications he was discharged from the flu wing
after two weeks, and recovered in the tent hospital
during the third week. The other dignitary was Judge
Gagnon. He was admitted with a right upper lobe
(RUL) pneumonia and with a large pleural effusion.
When the chest tube was inserted a full liter of
empyema was collected with a miraculous relief of his
shortness of breath (SOB). Over the next two weeks,
large volumes of bronchial secretions were expelled as

the chest tube was removed a week later. It was ironic that the one doctor who had been coerced to enlist in WW1 was the doctor who inserted the chest tube and saved the judge's life—Tom Hall MD.

Of note was another patient of Doctor Reinhart with longstanding end stage emphysema (COPD). He was admitted with bilateral viral pneumonia and had persistent hypoxia with very low oxygen levels. Being a DNR (do not resuscitate) he peacefully passed away in his sleep two days later.

One of the late admissions who was very ill was Winston Holmes. Again as Addie was the unit clerk she came to receive the patient. Recognizing him she said, "well here is the man who started all this. You bought my ranch and I married your doctor. This is Doctor Kelly, my husband, who will evaluate you. It being late March, you might be one of the last admissions we might get. But trust me, we are still providing the same care we did when we started in late January—but we are all a bit tired is all." True to expectations, he and another 32 patients were the last treated during the 1918 pandemic.

It was May 24th when the flu wing was officially closed after the last patients were discharged home as the rented hospital tent was returned. It was that night, while in their hot tub and the kids in bed, that Brad asked Addie to summarize some of the flu ward's statistics. Addie started by saying that the flu ward was closed but that did not mean that businesses and factories were all open since many workers were still recovering at home but not yet able to work. She then got to the statistics.

"We had a total of 271 patients admitted from January 21 to May 24. 40% had pneumonia, 40% had dehydration with or without pneumonia, 10% had strokes, 10% had reversible multi-organ failure, and we had a total of 12 deaths—2 were expected end-stage chronic diseases, 5 were sudden fatal unresponsive cardiac arrests compared to 22 of 27 successful resuscitations, 3 were hypoxia from severe pneumonia, and 2 were uncontrollable diabetes with fatal ketoacidosis and coma." "So that is 12 out of 271, or a mortality of +- 4%." "Correct!"

"I assume that our discharges did not all go home without some acquiring a long-term disability. If that is the case what are the disabilities?" "Well the stroke victims went home with multiple paralyzed extremities, or with loss of speech. The cardiac complications of CHF, arrythmias, and angina all continued and will be cared for by our medical doctors. The surgical patients all healed their chest tube procedures. The pneumonia patients all improved and it will take months to see if any get permanent lung scarring or other pulmonary complications."

Addie then asked, "Will you tell me why we only had four graduate nurses come down with the flu out of some 50 people working on the influenza victims?" "Influenza has been present for years and most of us older medical workers were exposed years ago. Today we all had natural immunity except for 19-year-olds out of training. Fortunately they all had minor cases and were soon back at work."

Brad then added, "that was a good summary and I especially liked the 4% mortality. Now how much did it cost us to take care of these 271 patients?" Addie was so surprised that she slipped and went under the surface. After recovering she said, "Bradly E Kelly MD, since when do you want to know our costs—that is all about MONEY." "Well this is a special event that was advertised as a free service, so we really need to know what it cost us, heh?" "Ok, well I don't have the exact figures since we never conducted an exact accounting for free care. But let's do a realistic analysis. Each sick patient spent at least two weeks in the hospital—flu wing and tent. Angus told me that an average day charge would be $7 a day. With that in mind multiply $7 by at least 14 days and you get +- $98 per patient. Now multiply that by 271 and you get +-$26,500. Now add the cost of food for patients and staff's three meals a day and add a few unrecognized expenses and you are probably around $30,000." "I see, well that likely empties our hospital reserve account doesn't it?" "Yep!" "Well let me think about this and maybe we'll apply for some financial relief from our city council since we did work to save the town taxpayers, heh?" "Sure let's try it, there isn't anything to lose, is there?"

*

It was a week later that the Duo was invited to the regular weekly council meeting. Present were Mayor Monroe, Judge Gagnon, Murdock Hatfield, Dumas Gregory, and the other council members. President Hatfield started the meeting. "Well Doctor Kelly I enjoyed your note which said 'enclosed is an estimate of $30,000 which was our cost to care for 271 local and county residents. Would you care to make a small donation to defray some of our costs? Thank you!'"

There was a long pause as President Hatfield said, "well we the council and others believe that we should help you defray some costs. So the council voted to give you this draft for $5,000 as a token of our appreciation for caring for us without ever charging a single resident. That was very noble. After another pause, Judge Gagno stood and said, "as county judge, I have authorized a county contribution of another $5,000 as our thanks from our taxpayers." The

Duo was pleased to accept both donations and was about to get up to leave when Dumas Gregory put his hand up.

"You may not know this, but you all took care of my second wife who registered under a false name. She to this day was amazed how some fifty people were working together to get everyone home. Well my wife had pneumonia and was pounded on for two weeks. She came home after a total of three weeks and is still talking about the care she got including the home cooked meals. For this reason I am making my contribution of $20,000—like a tip it is not returnable, heh?"

*

Sadly the flu wing was closed till it would again be needed. It took many months to return to normal hospital activities. Looking back it was a combination of events during 1918 and 1919 that again brought the hospital to 100% occupancy. The first event that reactivated the busy operating rooms was the request for delayed tubal-ligations--delayed because of the fear that influenza could be deadly on newborns. Now that the worst of the flu had passed, moms wanted to be sterilized before they stopped nursing their last baby and again became fertile.

The second was the well-advertised warning that prohibition would begin in January 1920. This was one of the triggers that caused the returning war veterans to rebel. Young men realized that they had lived thru a terrible trench war and an influenza pandemic. Now being home they were going to celebrate their survival by drinking, partying, driving fast cars, fornicating, using drugs, and shooting off ammo needlessly. It didn't take a genius to see what the results of such behavior would be. Over weeks promiscuous men and women would appear in the doctor offices with gonorrhea, alcohol hepatitis and bleeding stomachs from rotgut whiskey.

The worst occurrence was trauma from car accidents because of drinking and driving. Collisions were common with utility poles, other head-on vehicles, and even collisions with pedestrians. Common injuries were fractures, facial lacerations, liver tears, ruptured spleens, and contused or ruptured intestines. It seemed that pedestrians ended up the worst-off with life threatening injuries for all ages. It was so bad that surgeons, nurse anesthetists, and OR nurses would stay in the ER during evenings and all weekends to treat these cases or prep them for the OR. It was not unusual at 2AM to find both operating rooms conducting major life saving operations. Unfortunately, as with any high-speed car accident, young men and women were often DOA (dead on arrival), which only caused the dedicated ER staff to be somewhat demoralized.

As the woes of the times continued, another earth-shattering awareness raised the Duo's eyebrows.

*

It was June 1919 and school was out. The Duo was perplexed to see their 12-year-old son, Jimmy and their 11-year-old daughter, Dottie more interested in watching dad, from the OR watchtower, doing an operation, and spending more time reading mom and dad's nursing and surgical textbooks than going outside and playing with the other doctor's kids. The Duo let it all pass till the kids brought up the subject themselves.

It was family supper time. The kids and dad were sitting at the dinner table while mom was stirring a beef stew and waiting for bread to warm up. It had become customary for the kids to make up a daily list of medical words that needed pronunciation and explanation as mom and dad would explain them while sitting in the parlor AFTER SUPPER. This day, Dottie could not wait as she blurted out, "what is an enema?"

Since the Duo had always answered their questions, Addie said, "It is a bag full of hot soapy water that is attached to a tube that is inserted in … and relieves … !" There was total silence in the kitchen as Dottie finally said, "eeeeekkk. That does it, now I am absolutely certain that I do not want to be a nurse like mom. I want to be a doctor. I am as smart as Jimmy and I know I can do it." Brad kept the conversation going by asking, "what kind of doctor do you want to be?" "I want to be a medical doctor like Doc Reinhart and Tisdale. I want to write 'pre-script-ions' like they do by writing medicine names on a pad with their name on top. Then wait days to see if their patient gets better. My name will be Dorothy A Kelly MD" Addie was still playing along when she asked Jimmy, "what about you Jimmy?" "I want to be a surgeon like dad and cut-cut-cut the disease out and not wait weeks to see if the patient gets better. I will also have my own pad like dad and my name will read James B Kelly MD- Surgeon."

Brad was somewhat lost for words as Addie saved the day. "Well do you know how long it takes to be a doctor after high school graduation?" With negative nods Addie said, "by the time you all get to medical school it will be four years for Dottie and likely six years for Jimmy." Dottie added, "I am smart and ahead of my class, I bet you that I will skip 8th grade and be in high school with Jimmy. The Duo was about to leave the subject when Brad asked Dottie, "what happens if you get married and your name changes to say Smith instead of Kelly?" Dottie stood up and said, "Jimmy already solved that dilemma,

my name would then be Dorothy A Kelly-Hall MD,"
Addie said, "as in Doc Hall's son Eric—Jimmy's best
friend?"

"Why of course, didn't you know?" Addie had now
passed from perplexed to shocked as she said, "and
you Jimmy, who are you going to marry?" "Doctor
Norwood's daughter, Susie, for sure!" Brad dared
ask, "and where will you be practicing medicine and
surgery?" Jimmy quickly answered, "why where
Kellys practice, The Kelly Memorial Hospital of
Amarillo, Texas, heh?" Addie nonchalantly added,
"well that is good to know, now Brad please say grace
as the stew is ready."

That night, while in bed, Addie asked, "no one ever
warned me that being a parent could be so stressful.
Now what do we do about our two precocious kids?"
"Well, unless I am mistaken, it looks like the apple
may not fall far from the tree. Anyways, let's not
breach that subject again, but we allow them to read
our textbooks, we continue explaining the words each
night, and even let them watch the operating room
while in the tower. Besides, I don't think we should

push them going outside to play with the Hall boy or Norwood gal, for who knows what could happen?" Addie threw her pillow at Brad and uttered, "spoken like a man!"

CHAPTER 12

The Roaring 20's and Beyond

1920

It was 1920 and four kids entered high school together—to include Jimmy, Dottie, Eric, and Susie, of course. As Dottie had predicted she had skipped 8th grade and was right up there in medical knowledge. It was no surprise that the four would get together and talk about medicine. Eric had already said he wanted to be a surgeon and be Jimmy's partner, as Susie was going to be a medical doctor and be Dottie's partner. Despite the kids planning, the Duo knew they were young and anything could happen in four years. So Brad's approach was, "we don't discourage them but we don't encourage anything either" This time Addie said, "well what will be will be. Personally, I think our kids chose perfect mates and not so bad a profession to boot, heh?"

1920 Amarillo was in a state of disorder. To start things off, the banks wanted to get back into the business of loaning money now that the war and pandemic were over. Their likely targets were the unemployed male veterans. Hoping the young men would start up new businesses, they loaned anyone of them sizeable loans. So the young had pockets full of cash and a yearning to spend it on women, illegal alcohol, cars, guns, and one party after another.

Amidst these 'roaring times,' Addie was trying to maintain a hospital census above 50% occupancy while the surgeons were faced with requests for tubal-ligations in young single women without children. These were liberal times and without birth control beyond using condoms, women were seeking back street abortions with a high incidence of serious infections. So with the entire medical staff of doctors voting 8 to 1, the general surgeons agreed to perform these procedures with a strict release of liability for themselves and the hospital. The applicant for an irreversible sterilization had to sign the release form as her signature was witnessed by two independent observers, and counter signed by the hospital attorney.

The real change in the hospital protocol was the training of RNs to start the IVs with the new long-term cannulas. Every doctor spent his share of time showing nurses how to properly do the procedure. Starting with all the ER nurses, they then progressed to pre-op, then recovery, and finished with all ward charge nurses and night supers—plus three shifts a day. It was a massive undertaking but was worth it to free Doctor Greene and surgeons of the burden. In addition, a new phlebotomy RN with natural talents in locating deep veins, was trained to do most of the outpatient and inpatient drawings. As a back-up was one of the four technicians now doing laboratory tests. Doctor Greene was now free to be a real pathologist, an EKG technician/expert, and an X Ray expert in reading films. Despite his busy schedule, he had a new diagnostic machine in mind that was slowly appearing in the larger hospitals all over the country.

It was the end of year meeting with the medical staff (doctors) when Addie informed the doctors that something had to be done to increase the 50% census if the hospital was to survive. It was clear that people had not yet recovered from the war and epidemic, as they were also not adjusting well with prohibition and the free style liberal living attitudes. To every doctor's surprise, Addie had the answer. "You doctors need to specialize to draw patients from neighboring New Mexico, Oklahoma, and Colorado as we increase our catchment area from Amarillo to +- 250 miles in all three directions—north, east, west as south was covered by Dallas.

*

1921

Doctor Greene was first to respond to Addie's shocking request. He had taken the time to investigate when the new X Ray machine would be available, and to meet its arrival in three months, he decided to take an 8-week course at Dallas Medical Center in the science of live imaging—fluoroscopy. With a barium swallow, that would add diagnostic pictures of the esophagus, stomach, and small intestines— to help diagnose esophageal strictures, stomach ulcers, cancer, small intestine adhesions, and more. With a barium enema, it would add pictures of the entire large intestine from rectum to the appendix— allowing diagnosis of colon cancer, diverticulitis, abscesses, colitis, bowel obstruction, adhesions, and many more.

While away, a locum-tenens from Austin was hired to do Doctor Greene's duties. At the same time, Addie would be sending advertisements to every newspaper in the hospital's catchment area—as far as Albuquerque to the west, Oklahoma City to the east, and Pueblo to the north. Yes, in the Roaring 20s, hospitals and doctors advertised. The key ad to this live X Ray was "diagnosis without exploratory surgery."

When he returned to Amarillo, Doctor Greene brought back a new 'portable' chest/abdomen/ extremity X Ray machine, a new acumen in reading all X Rays, and the ability to operate a live fluoroscopic machine and interpret the static pictures it produced. It took a month but telegrams started coming in from surrounding doctors and private individuals for these live studies. Addie was adamant, "to promote more of these ordered studies, then every effort should be made to send the study's results to the referring doctors but that individuals requesting such studies would be seen by a surgeon before the study was done—thereby keeping the patients in this hospital if surgery was next to follow."

Another event that occurred in the hospital was when Doctors Reinhart and Tisdale opened an intensive care (ICU) and cardiac care unit (CCU) in the medical ward. Sequestered from the medical ward hubbub, the unit cared for the critically ill medical and cardiac patients. With the addition of new meds, the mortality of such patients was falling.

The most appreciated national discovery was that of injectable insulin in the treatment of the death sentence 'SUGAR DIABETES.' Patients were quick to learn how to inject themselves. Some patients who were still afraid of needles, and just could not do it, were given an auto injector where the loaded syringe was placed in the injector and all the patient had to do was pull the trigger.

At the end of 1921, the occupancy was up to 75% and outpatient income was drastically increased from the use of fluoroscopy. The surgeons were reminded that the improved survival of ICU and CCU patients had a significant effect in increasing hospital income.

*

1922

Doctor Hall had been reading current surgical changes in managing kidney stones, bladder tumors, prostate enlargement/occlusion. It was clear that new instruments allowed visualization of bladder contents, ureter stone extraction, and a trans-urethral-resection of the prostate (TURP) without the dreaded suprapubic prostatectomy. After making arrangements, he returned to Dallas for a three-month training program in the new field called 'Urology.' While he was there, he met with the salesmen and ordered all the equipment to practice this new field.

Concurrently, Addie was busy on the telegraph advertising this new specialty. The Urology moto was, 'why suffer with painful dribbling urination or stones, we can clear the way with noninvasive surgery.'

When Tom came back, he was faced with a ready list of waiting patients wanting a prostate procedure without open surgery. He also came back with a warning to the other doctors. "Start reading the financial section of national papers, for investment methods are heading for a bad ending." It was weeks later that the doctors were all convinced that the banks would fail with their uncollectable loan repayments. So their hard- earned money was in peril if left in their bank accounts.

The doctors started to have private financial meetings and when they learned that investors were buying stocks on margin, the bulk of the doctors not only withdrew their accounts in cash but placed the funds in waterproof/fireproof hidden safes. Many doctors decided to start buying land, specially building lots on the outskirts of town since population growth was a guarantee during the 20s robust cattle market.

The value of a Urologist at the Kelly Memorial Hospital spread like wildfire and at the end of 1922, the census was up to almost 90 %.

*

1923

That year included revelations for the Kelly family. The two high school sweetheart couples were now in their junior year as the summer was approaching. One memorable night, they managed to get the Kellys, the Halls, and the Norwoods together for a family meeting. It was Jimmy elected to represent the two couples. "You all know that the four of us have coupled after years of being playmates and friends. Well we are now in love and are asking you the privilege of stepping out (dating) privately without being under the gun of a chaperone." It was clear that the comment hit the parents like a sledgehammer.

Dottie could see that and decided to clear the air. "Now really mom and dad, you raised us right so it is time to trust us. Besides if Eric and I decide to be intimate, as it will happen, there is not an army that could stop us. Heck, we could do it behind the back yard's big oak tree, heh?" Most of the parents were choking up a laugh that was trying to escape. Addie cut the tension when she said, "Brad, make sure you have that oak tree cut down no later than next week!" The place erupted and was in shambles as Addie got up, went to Susie, hugged her, and said, "welcome to our family, we love you, but be nice to Jimmy. She then went to Eric and hugged him as she added, "if you hurt my baby girl, you will never walk straight again but if you are good then the benefits will be plenty. The rest of the parents then got up and there were plenty of handshakes, hugs, and tears to wash the entire floor. It was Eric who said, "mom, I am not leaving you and dad, I am trying to add a daughter-in-law to our family—and maybe grand children in the far future, heh?"

The other Kelly revelation was when Brad admitted that he had silently for years wished he knew how to perform vascular surgery. Discussing it with Addie he said, "we need better ways to repair lacerated arteries and with an innovative vascular surgeon in Dallas, I hear he has developed a technique for cleaning out carotid arteries to prevent strokes in patients who have transient ischemic attacks (TIA). He has also made some synthetic tubes to make bypasses along the femoral or popliteal arteries. This is something I would like to learn."

Brad spent 8 weeks in Dallas as Addie advertised, "if you have stroke warnings, don't wait till paralyzed—get your carotids cleaned out." It took a while but doctors were first to respond and request that their patients have the endarterectomies done by Doctor Kelly.

The summer of 1923 was a busy summer for the precocious Kelly kids and lovers. Looking ahead to school after high school and needing money for dating; all four kids became orderlies in the hospital and on different shifts—of course. The year closed with the hospital hitting a 100% occupancy rate since pre-war golden years.

*

1924

The four kids graduated from high school with high honors. With four applications to Dallas Medical Center Medical School, and with a dispensation for Dorothy who was 17 and a year short of adulthood, the Quad proudly presented themselves for a medical school entrance examination and interview. After a two-hour written exam, the Quad was introduced to the admissions officer, the renowned Karl Huxley MD.

With all four applicants before Doctor Huxley, the interview was started with Doctor Huxley saying, "it is almost as it was in 1905. Before me I see Cindy Norwood, Tom Hall, and the infamous Addie and Brad Kelly. Besides that, I am proud to say that you all ace'd the entrance exam. How did you do that? You actually know more medicine than our first-year medical students." Jimmy answered, "because we have been studying together for four years." There was a pause as Doc Huxley said to Dorothy, "and you Miss Kelly, you are too young to enter medical school but because you are the grandchild of our famous teachers and Addie and Brads daughter, we are making an exception. Now if you are willing to start your studies in September we need to set up some housing choices. I am thinking that with you gals all with an engagement ring that we will be providing some couples' housing, heh?"

Tom answered, "yes Doctor, we have a double wedding ceremony planned for August 15." Doctor Huxley smiled as he pulled out his wedding invitation sent from Addie and Brad. After another hour of friendly banter, the two couples were given their entry papers, their apartment keys, and sent to the bookstore so they could pick up their textbooks ahead of the rush. As they were leaving Jimmy and Eric handed Doctor Huxley a total of $14,000 for each the gals four years and each the guys six years. That night each couple spent the night in their apartment before returning to Amarillo to their summer orderly jobs and their wedding.

*

1925

Doctor Scanlon had always enjoyed treating fractures. Now he was aware that there were new stainless-steel hardware, techniques, and pinning of fractured hips. Fractured hips had always been a nightmare to treat as without long pins to secure the hip, patients would have to be put on 2-3 months on complete bedrest. This was not well tolerated and complications would usually cause 75% of those patients to not survive—especially those over 50 years of age. So Donald Scanlon spent 4 months on the new orthopedic ward. While waiting for fractured hips, open fractures, unstable fractures; the surgeons repaired the many rotator cuff tears, knee torn cartilage meniscus, and reattaching torn knee collateral ligaments.

While Doctor Scanlon was away, Doctor Titus had to be hospitalized because of severe hip arthritis from rheumatoid arthritis. Realizing that his years of attending long hours at the operating table were short lived, it was Addie who could see the need for this doctor to continue practicing medicine as the first Kelly Memorial Hospital ER doctor.

When Doctor Scanlon returned and set up an actual orthopedic department, the hospital census was at the busting stage and complicated by a boom in the local population to +- 30,000 people. There was talk that it was time to open the dormant 'flu ward.' With 1926 around the corner the medical staff got together and a major surgical overhaul was set into motion for January of 1926

*

1926--1927

There was talk that three surgeons, with the population boom, would not be able to provide all the surgical care this community would need. Then Doctor Titus came to work in the ER. Suddenly the three surgeons were free of suturing interruptions, minor fractures, working up patients with potentially surgical problems, or even doing and reviewing X Rays. In short it was a help for everyone including the medical doctors who would benefit from fully evaluated patients before admission. To everyone's pleasure, Doctor Titus's diagnoses were always on the money.

The big event of the year was a major surgical renovation. The surgical suite was torn up and converted to more general surgery beds. The surgical suite was moved to the entrance of the flu wing. There, a new style OR design was used to construct four operating rooms, new more modern sterilizing rooms, anesthetic agent storage, cleaning sinks, supervisor office, storage, ladies changing and bathrooms, nurses' lounges, a doubly enlarged recovery room, and an enlarged doctors' lounge with showers. The entire surgical suite was air conditioned. The flu wing was spruced up and covered into a specialized post-op surgical ward for orthopedic, urological, and vascular surgery—including trained nurses in the care of these complicated patients.

By the end of the year, the hospital census was over 125% occupancy made possible by opening the flu wing for the new specialized post-op patients.

*

1928

The hospital had been open and operational for 22 years and needed a facelift. With the profits of the past five years, it was time to spend some money and obtain a cosmetic appearance of modern hospitals. Addie was placed in charge. Her first step was to invite a modern medical designer from Dallas Medical Center. Aloysius Abernathy arrived with a team of professional renovators. Addie had arranged for Mike Walters to be present.

"Mister Abernathy, my husband and I, the hospital owners, are responding to our medical staff who want our hospital to look like Dallas General." "We can make that happen but most 100 bed hospitals that take on the modern look end up paying over $20,000." "We can pay that much as long as you include Mike to do some of the work, and you do this as quickly as possible. We cannot close this place down to give it a facelift, heh?" "We can do that. So let me walk about with my team and Mike and we'll meet later today to go over the changes needed."

It was 4PM when the renovators met with the Duo. Aloysius started with a whopper. "This entire hospital, minus central supply, needs new flooring. The rubber tiles are worn and ends are lifting up. Central supply is excluded since the tiles are faring well and to remove the shelves and thousands of supplies will take too long—for no one but the purchasing agent goes in there and the door is always locked."

Brad added, "so what would you replace it with?" "Same thing as is in the Dallas General. A hard tile mortared to the concrete. It is a mosaic of brown, grey, green and some red/black. It is easy to keep clean, hides the dirt, and is anti-skid. Plus the foot-wide perimeter edging solid color will vary depending on the different wards and the mop boards will be the same color as the foot-wide edging." Brad added, "been in the Dallas General lately and I agree that the floors look fantastic."

Aloysius then said, "I have decided to present the changes in the two medical and surgical wards. That way you will get a gist of what things should look like. Here is the list:

MEDICAL/SURGICAL WARDS

1. The nurses' station, unit clerk desk, pharmacy, and nurses' lounge/bathroom need to move from the back of the ward to the front. That will free up a lot of square footage for storage—the greatest need according to the charge nurses.

2. You need to sacrifice two patient rooms to accomplish #1.

3. The unit clerk's desk will now become a standing counter to do her work and direct visitors—that's why the greeting needs to be as the visitors enter—not after they stopped at every room to find their family or friends.

4. All the beds must go. We now have beds with waterproof mattresses and automatic bed position changers that patient and nurse can operate. The up and down siderails are gone. Instead they flip up into a half position or full elevation—again operated by patient or nurse.

5. All patient bathrooms will be modernized. The ceiling high water tank is gone. The porcelain

toilets have their own tanks, and the sinks are modern.

6. We are adding an over the bed extra light—per nursing's request.

7. That dark paneling must go. We now have a light oak that brightens the room and is still washable.

8. Visitor chairs will recline in case a family member plans to sleep in the patient's room.

9. All privacy curtains need to be changed.

10. Nurses want a second infectious disease isolation room.

11. Rollaway cots are now being used when a patient is over- demanding and a family member can be useful."

Aloysius paused and looked at the Duo. With full smiles, he knew that they approved. He then said, "keeping these changes as universal, I will now cover other parts of the hospital with specific changes."

SPECIALTY SURGICAL WARD

"The two multi-patient wards will be converted into private hospital rooms—a current trend in new hospitals. Otherwise, the other new ward changes will be included here. The single/double rooms will remain a convertible option."

DINING ROOM

"This room needs a real overhaul. New square tables for four but can be joined to make a conference table. New chairs, floor, walls to be changed to the new sheetrock and painted in bright pastel colors. It should be a pleasant place for the staff to rest and take refreshments."

KITCHEN

"With an all-alloy kitchen we would only change the cooking back wall, the serving counter, exhaust fans, and of course the floor."

VISITOR BATHROOM

"Everything needs changing, stalls, toilets, sinks, and we'll add men's urinals with backsplashes."

OR SUITE

"Seeing it was just moved and patterned like the Dallas General; it does not need to be changed. But we will add new flooring."

ENTRANCE SQUARE

"We need to get rid of the drab appearance. This is where visitors get their first impression. Other than knowing we are enlarging the coffee shop, trust me when I say that we will make this an 'OMG' room."

ICU/CCU

"Wow, that place looks just like Dallas General, your doctors did a nice job duplicating a modern unit. But the flooring must go."

MATERNITY WARD

"Like the other wards, this place needs a complete overhaul to include post-partum rooms, nursery, and labor/delivery. Plus it needs the new delivery chairs/tables as well as the second room with a new operating table. Now we were told that there are no ladies due for the next two weeks. So with our teams and Mike's carpenters working 24 hours a day, we'll have that one completed before the next lady in labor presents herself."

NURSING AND DAYCARE

"We noticed that the nursing room has been frequently changed and it is fine the way it is—except the floor. The daycare gets a lot of use and will be upgraded to include the furniture and colorful walls."

DOCTORS' WING

"I am not going to mince my words. This is where patients see the doctors and get their first impression. As it is now, it is antiquated and we will turn it into a modern location and include the abused waiting room. Although we must start with the maternity ward, I assure you that the doctors' wing will be next to join the current century."

EMERGENCY ROOM

"We are aware that you have used the new name since the emergency department is not a ward but a room. Specifically, the dividing curtains must go. We will add permanent walls for privacy and a unit clerk/head nurse counter at the private entrance. The waiting room has to be added to separate it from the doctor's wing waiting room. Doctor Titus will now have a private office and the fracture room will be widened to allow entry of the portable X Ray unit. All beds and stretchers will be new. The pharmacy will have better locks for narcotic meds. A second trauma room will be added with extra overhead lights. Cabinets will hold IV bottles and tubing. Trust me when I say that we will make it look just like a big city trauma center."

"Well that does it. My team and Mike have agreed how the jobs will be assigned and my accountant has a firm figure of $18,000 +-$2,000. How he can get a reliable figure this quick is beyond me but he is rarely wrong."

Brad looked at Aloysius and said, "today is September 25. Assuming the last lady delivers Oct 1st can you guarantee us that you will be done and gone by December 1st." "Absolutely and for every day we work past December 1, we will refund you $100 a day. And I assure you we rarely have to pay that penalty, heh?" After signing the contract and giving the renovators a deposit of $10,000, the Duo retired to their office.

Brad was first to speak, "Ok, then on December 20 we are going to have the biggest open house that will out do the one in +-1905!" Addie looked at Brad as she said, "and I suppose that you expect me to put on that gala?" "Well yes, organizing it, but you don't have to be the entertainment, heh?" "Now tell me why you chose December 20?" "Because I already checked and the four kids will be here to participate during their Xmas holiday. Actually it is appropriate since we are doing these renovations for them, heh?" "But dear, they are not scheduled to finish their surgical training till August of 1930, and that is +- 18 months from now, and you know the gals are not leaving their husbands to start their practice 18 months early and some 300 miles from their better half. They are now working in a medical clinic and are supporting their husbands. So, why are we rushing to do this during the fall of 1928?"

There was a long pause as Brad said, "because the economists are predicting that the stock market will crash within the next year. If that happens, there won't be any supplies to do the renovations. Plus, no one seems to know how long the resultant depression will last. So, the only solution is to make hay when the sun shines. We renovate now when we can, heh?" "Without a doubt, you are again right, my dear husband!"

*

As promised, the renovations were done by December 1ˢᵗ. Addie was now placing ads in the local and outlying newspapers that read like:

> Welcome to our open house on December 20. We have renovated the hospital and you won't recognize it. Enjoy free hot dogs, bearpaw pastries, coffee, and tea all day. Free raffles every 15 minutes for medical supplies. The top prize is $100 to be drawn at 4PM. Come and meet some old friends who will soon be our four new physicians. Doctors will hold discussions to explain the new surgical departments of orthopedics, urology, and vascular surgery.

The ads appeared twice a week till the actual open house took place. It was two days before the event when the three parents were waiting at the railroad terminal. As often as the parents traveled to Dallas to spend a weekend with their kids, this was a special meeting as the docs would be presented to the locals and dignitaries.

The private greeting was a personal event. Once the tears dried out, Addie said, "well what do you say we give you all a private tour of our new digs." While on route, Eric handed his dad a package. "What is this son?" "A gift from your old teachers in Urology. It is the new sulfa antibiotic that just came out. Use it prophylactically before instrumentation to prevent the dreaded 'Urosepsis!'

To see the Quad enter the 'square' was a fly trapping jaw dropping event. Ward by ward, the Quad recognized several resemblances to the Dallas General. Of course the gals were mostly interested in the ICU/CCU as the guys perused the well-organized surgical suite. After the other areas were covered it was Addie who said, "If everything goes well, by spring this entire hospital will be air conditioned!"

The last portion of the tour was the Doctors Wing. The Quad liked the design and furnishings in the office compared to the treatment rooms. When they got to the last rooms, Dottie and Susie started crying.

There in front of them were four door labels that read James B Kelly MD-Surgery, Eric T Hall MD-Surgery, Susan C Norwood-Kelly MD-Medicine, and Dorothy A Kelly-Hall MD-Medicine.

The public open house was a total success and the best part was the portion after the tour—getting to meet the new doctors. Some were old high school classmates, some were old merchant faces, and some were new locals and dignitaries. It was a tough time for the moms to let go their kids for another 18 months. Yet till the kids returned, a lot more needed to be done before the unknowing historic event of late 1929.

*

1929

The year was a productive one. The surgeons were as busy as they could be, referrals for elective surgery were plentiful in all three subspecialties. Private doctor incomes were off the wall because of the new specialty surgeries along with standard surgeries performed on locals. Doc Kelly was the expert in artery repairs as well as doing carotid endarterectomies to prevent strokes. Doc Hall was removing enlarged prostates, removing bladder tumors, and pulling out stones stuck in the ureters—all through the cystoscope and the resectoscope. Doc Scanlon was using a revolutionary procedure to pin fractured hips and cutting down recovery days by months. Now using stainless steel screws and plates there were no more 'failed unions' and 'nonhealing fractures.'

Medicine was good and the hospital was high in the black. However the economy and stock market were near peril. After a heavy selloff for several days, the stock market crashed on October 29, 1929. Overnight, elective surgery and out of town referrals came to an abrupt stop. Suicides and failed attempted suicides filled the ER. Empirically, the nursing staff had to be laid off to match the inpatient census. It became a rotating system that allowed most nurses some weekly survival income. With the country entering a great depression, the hospital Benefactor Fund would be a lifesaver for many families—including hospital staff.

*

It was one of those nights when the Duo ended up with a tub meeting. Addie started, "the talk around is that in 1905, when a nurse was sent home, they would still make full pay. Now either you worked or there was no pay. heh?" "Yes I know what it was like back then, but they all had a guaranteed salary then. Today, we have no idea how long this 'great depression' will last. Heh, there are lines for one meal a day, no one has any money, and there are no jobs. We are having to do surgery without pay. I know we have plenty of cash in our safes, but still we have to be frugal and not spend any money that we don't have to if we want to keep this hospital afloat. I even told Angus that, when he spent the last $1,000 in the Benefactor Fund, that there wouldn't be any more deposits in the account. Times are tough and we have to meet the challenge in order to survive, heh?"

After the Xmas holidays, the Quad returned to Dallas. The gals had no work so volunteered in the Dallas General Hospital. The guys were now attendings and spent their days in the ER looking for cases or trauma to fill their OR times. To their surprise, the older town attendings did not have any business so started spending time in the ER sharing cases with the attending residents. It was now spring, and Jimmy and Eric decided that there were too many hungry local attendings competing for a few golden nuggets. The writing was on the wall, it was time to enter the world of practicing doctors and work with the experienced medical and surgical doctors as they entered the practice in Amarillo, Texas.

*

After another memorable tub meeting, Addie asked, "how do you feel about taking Eric and Jimmy under your wings?" "I know it is early but this is May and we would have done the same in August. At least both Doctors Tisdale and Reinhart are so tired that they are happy to see Susie and Dottie come early. We will manage. Tom and I have agreed that the guys will do whatever surgical cases come around, and that he and I will assist our kids. Heck, that is going to be a riot, heh?" Addie was serious when she said, "with this depression likely lasting years, it is clear that our children will be responsible for taking over the hospital and bringing it into the next decades, heh?" "Yes, right again, my dear wife!"

There was a long pause when it was obvious that both Brad and Addie were woolgathering or reminiscing. It was Brad who spoke first, "I guess we can say WE HAVE HAD OUR TURN." Addie was defiant as she said, "is that enough, I know we built the hospital, started a productive practice, and got the hospital thru a pandemic and a world war. Does that mean this is the end?" After another pause Brad added, "we are both in our late 40s with years of experience and a nice retirement income. I am certain that I will continue to use my surgical skills and to pass as much as I can to the two new surgeons. You will also continue to do the administrative work and I am certain that one of those girls will slowly take over that responsibility from you. That is an expected natural course of events but only time will tell what the future will bring, heh?" "For sure my husband!"

***

The End

See author's note

AUTHOR'S NOTE

I am certain that our readers are aware that the ending can be a finality or be set up for a sequel with the next generation of doctors during the 30s, 40s, and 50s. So plan to follow these characters' lives thru the difficult times of WWII, the polio epidemic, and the changing developments in medicine and surgery.

Richard M Beloin MD

ABOUT THE AUTHOR

The author is a retired medical physician who, with his wife of 50+ years, spend their summers in Vermont and their winters in the Texas Rio Grande Valley.

Early in his retirement before 2016, he enjoyed his lifelong hobby of guns and shooting. He participated in the shooting sports to include Cowboy Action Shooting, long range black powder, USPSA, trap, and sporting clays. At the same time he wrote a book on shooting a big bore handgun, a desk reference on volume reloading, and two fictions on the cowboy shooting sports. Since 2016 he has become a prolific writer of western fiction circa 1870-1900—the Cowboy Era.

It was during the Covid pandemic, in a self-imposed quarantine, that he wrote a dozen books. A newly adopted writing genre covered three phases: a bounty hunter's life as a Paladin with his unique style of bringing outlaws to justice, a romantic encounter that changed his life, and the building of a lifelong enterprise that would support the couple's future when they hanged up their guns—as each enterprise is different from book to book.

Although three of his books have a sequel, the others are all a standalone publication. With a dozen books ready for publication in 2023, and to keep the subject matter varied, this author elects to publish them out of sequence.

I hope you enjoy reading my books, and if you do, please leave a comment on the seller's web site.

Richard M Beloin MD

AUTHOR'S PUBLICATIONS

Non fiction

Fiction in modern times

Western fiction (circa 1880-1900+)
(The Bounty Hunter/Entrepreneur series)

Western Fiction (circa 1873-1933)
(The Bounty Hunter, Romance
and entrepreneur series)

Western Fiction (circa 1900-1930)
Romance and Entrepreneur